good deed rain

Books by Allen Frost

Ohio Trio
Bowl of Water
Another Life
Home Recordings
The Mermaid Translation
The Selected Correspondence of Kenneth Patchen
The Wonderful Stupid Man
Saint Lemonade
Playground
Roosevelt
5 Novels
The Sylvan Moore Show
Town in a Cloud
A Flutter of Birds Passing Through Heaven:
    A Tribute to Robert Sund
At the Edge of America
Lake Erie Submarine
The Book of Ticks
I Can Only Imagine
The Orphanage of Abandoned Teenagers
Different Planet
Go with the Flow: A Tribute to Clyde Sanborn
Homeless Sutra
The Lake Walker
A Hundred Dreams Ago
Almost Animals
The Robotic Age
Kennedy
Fable
Elbows & Knees: Essays & Plays
The Last Paper Stars

The Last Paper Stars © 2019
Allen Frost, Good Deed Rain
Bellingham, Washington
ISBN 978-1-64516-991-8

Writing: Allen Frost
Cover Photos: Rustle Frost
Illustrations: Allen Frost
Apple: TFK!

"Only a fairy princess
could put it over now
and there ain't no such thing."

—W.C Fields
You're Telling Me (1934)

Credits:
How to Care for Your Monster, Norman Bridwell,
Scholastic Books, NY, 1970.

THE
LAST
PAPER
STARS

INTRODUCTION:

"So you want to own a monster? Many people do these days. You can bring a monster into your home. It's just a matter of finding one you like. This book will tell you how to get your monster, and how to keep him healthy and happy."

—How to Care for Your Monster

When I brought this manuscript to the island to work on, little did I know it had plans of its own. As soon as we reached the ferry terminal, it turned into another passenger. Suddenly the pages were Boris Karloff as the Frankenstein monster. We parked on the lower level and he followed me up the steep stairway and out onto the deck. The harbor lights shined in the black. The engine rumbled and the dark water hissed. He leaned into the wind with his hands on the rail. Out in the night we passed sleeping shapes of islands, some with secret mansions hidden in the firs. He reached for a bird that pedaled by. Clouds blanketed around a nearly full moon. Another ferry crossed our path. Rows of windows bright as a shrine. Of course he didn't mind being pulled along by the sea, but I left to get warm inside. I could see his silhouette out the window while I read the plaque about the Mosquito Fleet. A thousand steamships once traveled around Puget Sound. One more island and we were there.

No surprise, he didn't want to go about in the day. The town didn't interest him, the shops and the sidewalks and the smell of cinnamon. He made me stop the car at a dead cedar tree. Cormorants roosted all the way to the top. He liked the forest and he liked the sea. He would stare over the edge of the dock as if the deep jade water was a movie screen. A great big sky blue slice of cold.

When night returned, he was happy to be in those shadows again. We set out together and ahead of us a lamppost glowed. A funny sight in all these woods. It must be there for the moths. It's also like a phone booth that has called other creatures near.

I whistle when I see the fox. It turns and trots our way. I didn't expect that. It runs up as if I'm an old friend. It comes so close I could reach out and pet it. I talk to it and admire its fine orange coat. The eyes don't seem to recognize me though. We belong to different worlds. But as it orbits us another time, the pages flutter.

Most of this book I wrote 30 years ago, in the language of a 20 year old. No wonder Frankenstein appeared. He isn't precisely constructed. He is missing rivets and the seams are showing when he spins in circles with the fox, but he has that heart Frank Sinatra sings about. The fox knows. I tell my creation to follow. I've been with this story long enough. I can only do so much work on it before I let this book go.

Thanksgiving, 2018
Friday Harbor, San Juan Island

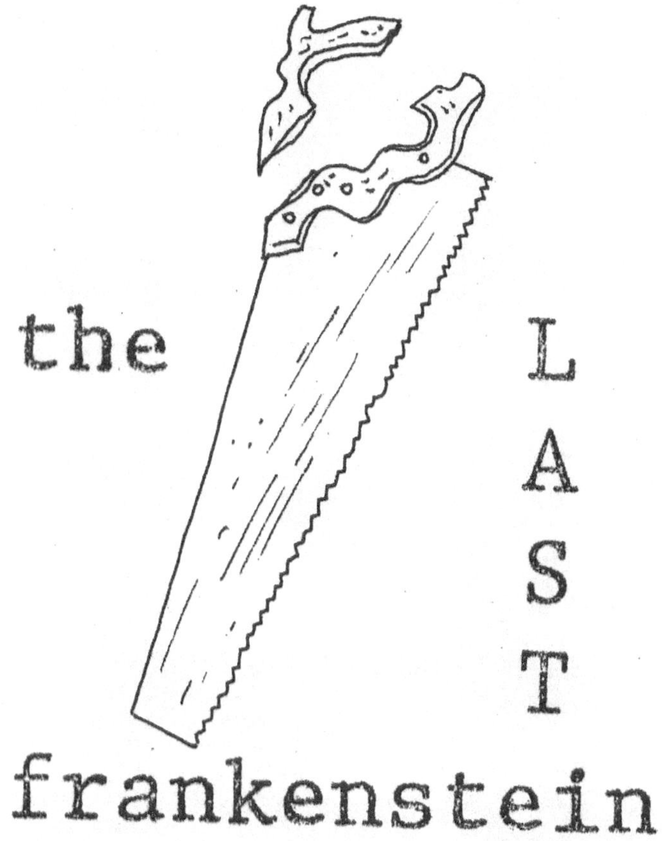
the
LAST
frankenstein

from original manuscript

Electricity

Doctor Frankenstein strung a long wire trail from a Shell gas station lot. This was all done in the darkest secrecy, not even the moon shined that night. There was only one attendant, in a yellow lit booth, attracting moths. He wore a blue and gray uniform with his name stitched on. He was staring at his feet, listening to the radio. It was a baseball game. He had no idea he was attracting lightning.

This was how Frankenstein was creating his monster. The conducting power of a minimum wage slave would be the spark for the work force of the future. Exchanging life for life, he could build the perfect human machine out of dead parts. It would never feel, it would never dream or want more.

He unspooled on through the field behind the distant Shell. Above him the black sky was boiling and as he stepped over a small creek, dragging an armful of wire, a bolt of lightning struck nearby. The storm was closing. Further into the forest, he had a house with a carport and a basement laboratory. Glass block glowed around the front door.

Frankenstein's experiment was brewing

underground. The cellar window was already open to the cool night so he tossed the last loop of wire inside. There was just enough left to reach the regenerator. Shadows took him into the backyard, to a storm door leading underground. Opening one of the slanted doors, he disappeared. He reached for the light switch and with its click he saw the whole room revealed, the walls of machinery and the human shape on an operating table in the center.

He turned switches and circuits and picture tubes glared. Ozone burned in the rumbling air. The lights blinked off and on with lightning and approaching thunder.

Back at the gas station a bolt of a million volts was about to strike. In the same instant it would create a crater, the life force would be carried like crazy through the cables.

There was bound to be damage to his monster's mind coming back from the dead. Things would be lost, the shock would splinter memories. But Dr. Frankenstein wondered how much the monster would need to know. The sky crashed. Electricity jumped into its body.

When the monster first opened its eyes, the world was upside down. But the room turned as it sat up and swung its legs over to the floor.

Dr. Frankenstein calmed the creature and in the days that followed, he taught it what it needed to know to survive. Language wasn't necessary for it, just an understanding of obeying orders. The creator showed it how to live, how to walk, how to hold things, how to work.

The monster shook at the sight of the blue spinning light on those wooden shelves. Dr. Frankenstein collected lightning in huge glass jars and he warned his monster that even though fire brought life, the power trapped circling in those jars could kill too. From the beginning, it was taught a fear of fire.

Sometimes Dr. Frankenstein let it explore outside, let it stagger out into the woods and tall trees. There, the monster could be allowed to forget the training for just that while before it returned to the house. When it went into the forest, it felt far away from everything and it would like to stand completely still so that it was like another quiet tree. And it could hold itself silent for hours and become a part of the moving, living and dying of the forest.

Out of the trees, as the land disappeared under asphalt roads and cement, the way was paved toward the city where it would work. Factory chimneys stood into the sky and poured out the smoke of everything they were making. From now on, the monster was told, this would be its home.

Minimum Wage

Maybe one day there would be robots in the workplace, but until that day Frankenstein's monster would have to do. Think of the money they would save! Here in the free world, home of the brave, it would work for free. It didn't need insurance policies or protective measures. It would work twelve hours a day in any form of minimum wage job. Given all the dead-end possibilities, breaking it in for the millions to come, the future could be served by the dead. America could be rich once again. If the Frankenstein solution was successful it had to be tested, so the monster was moved from place to place, from one job to another.

"When you arrive in the morning, you take your card and you stamp it in the time-clock. Then, before you leave, you stamp it again. This proves you were here."

It worked in a restaurant, behind swinging doors, scraping leftover food off into the garbage and it washed dishes clean in the sink.

"You should treat every one of our products

with the utmost respect. See yourself in every one of them. See that flag on the wall? I put that up there so every one of my workers will know what they're working for."

It worked in a warehouse, packing things into boxes with Styrofoam and paper. People showed it how to do things right. When it made a mistake, all the workers were called around to see what it did wrong.

"If you understand me, nod. Yes? Good. Here, take this bag of fries, see? Good. Now you pour this much into the strainer. Not all of them, they wouldn't all fit. Just this much, see? Good. Okay. Now you lower the fries into the hot oil and it cooks. Easy, right? Now, you try. Here's the bag. Remember, don't pour them all in. No, *more* than that! That's not enough for one person. Come on, more than that! Look! Like I did! It's not that hard to do! Most people catch on right away, it's so simple. Here, give me the fries! I'll show you again. This is how much to put in, see? Can you remember that? *This much*, see? Now here, you take it. What do you do next? No! No, you lower it into the oil! God, it's so easy! Like this—give it to me!

Look. See? Now they're cooking, right? Do you understand? Goddamn. You gotta be able to work fast. It's fast food here. See, we can probably get some more fries going now. Here, you try again and see if you can manage without me telling you how."

It worked in a cannery cutting fish with a sharp knife, laying their silver bodies tight into tins.

Because they didn't like the monster, there were rumors and words spoken behind its back. In the lunchroom, when it entered and sat down quietly in the corner, it could feel the weather change.

It worked at a parking garage, standing there in the cold watching cars move across the tar.

"All you need to do is take one of these and put it in the envelope. Okay? Here's a stack of envelopes and here's the inserts. There are more of them over there against the wall when you run out."

It worked as a cashier, but the money was confusing. A man from the reservation came in with three returnable cans, for a fifteen cent refund. The monster gave him all the money in the register.

"If you can't cut it, I want you to tell me right now. If you can't, you're just wasting my time. I won't tolerate that. You must be able to make a total commitment to this job. I demand perfection, nothing less. If you want to work for me, you'll follow my rules. Here's where you stand to watch them go by. If you see one that looks like this, it's a mistake. No customer would buy this. So you put it in this bin here. It's a reject."

A life of fragments when nothing had any purpose and the monster couldn't think. They'd show it what to do and it would perform. Years could pass like this…without it feeling a thing.

It worked sweeping streets, moving garbage from one end to the other, but all the junk kept piling up behind it again before it was through.

"We'll just say we saw it opening the cash

drawer. It's too dumb to prove it didn't take the money. This will be the easiest hundred bucks ever!" They watched the monster peeling vegetables, daydreaming, lost to all of this world, as they opened the cash register.

It worked for a while painting walls, but its balance on ladders wasn't good. It would fall and end up on the ground.

A small room cornered in a basement was where it spent the hours at night, trying to sleep. It was covered with a heavy blanket.

It worked on the conveyor belt at a small factory, putting together things made of plastic. It clipped together two separate pieces to become one and then it set this back on the track, to move it on to the next person. They all worked together against the clock.

"Now you show me how to do it. It's alright if you can't remember exactly. In a while you'll have it down pat. When I started, I wasn't perfect either, you know. It takes practice." She took his hands for him and placed them on the metal levers. "This one makes it go down, this one makes it go up…That's right…"

For hours that first week, she helped him and he didn't know why.

She would be standing there beside the machine in the morning when he arrived.

She would hold his hands and touch his shoulder and smile and talk all about herself while they worked. When she was so close, he even noticed how she smelled. To him she was like flowers around all that metal.

He wondered if he should try to talk to her. It kept him up all night thinking of how he should tell her. She gave him new things to think about.

But in the morning, instead of her there in her blue overalls, the boss was waiting for him. While he was told he was fired, he looked and he could see her faraway through the machines, separated from him by miles and miles of noise. She looked different, so distant she could have been someone else.

He wasn't even allowed to say goodbye to her. He had one last glance of her. Like someone seen between waves of vines and blackberry leaves.

Days became slow, twenty four hours long, the gray light of getting up to go to work and then coming back. It was all a machine, waking to an alarm and falling asleep in front of the TV. He was spinning out of control, down.

They had him starting to see himself as people must see him. He was a monster. Dr. Frankenstein had never shown his monster that mirror—he feared what might happen.

Dr. Frankenstein was worried his creation was failing. Something had gone wrong. He knew why. It was the creature's heart. "That was the point of a heart—so it would love what it was doing, not miss what it couldn't have." There was a reason he had to show it such terrible things—to see if it could survive…With or without a heart, life would be hard.

Flowers

Someone at work told him he should go to the circus, that he could even find friends there, people just like himself. They laughed, but he didn't know the joke. He stared at the advertisement picturing a woman only two feet tall.

They were right though—he didn't even need a ticket—he was allowed to walk right through the gates like he belonged there.

The field was filled with tents and blinking lights and rides and booths and people running and wandering all throughout. He laughed at the clowns and hid from the tigers in their cages, growling at him.

Watching someone try to knock down metal milk bottles, throwing badly and missing, he felt his shirt sleeve pulled. He turned and there was a man in a suit and tie.

"A living monster! You're a living monster! It's incredible!" The man yanked some money out of an inside vest pocket and offered it all, "Look, twenty dollars if you'll join our Monster Hall of Fame for the night. Don't pass me up, you're a natural!"

He felt the money go into his palm while he

stared and he felt his feet moving underneath him as he was walked to a stand hit with bright spotlights.

"Here, don't move. I'll be back at closing and you can go home. You look great!"

A green light was shined up onto his face. He looked down next to him and there was a purple dodo, worn out in a glass case. But he could tell now this wasn't what he wanted. He was getting scared by all the people passing him, pointing. He had to find somewhere to hide his fear. His eyes went across the crowd. He rubbed his hands together over the seams and held back a scream.

That's when he saw her. She wasn't even that far away.

She didn't need a sign or lights to attract him. The Amazing Glass Eating Girl had a booth with green drapes pulled aside. She swallowed glass like nothing could hurt her insides.

She smiled for the crowd then her eyes went into him, opening a door into his dead soul and there was life turned on inside of him all of a sudden. Some kind of electricity lit him again. All this time she had been there and his hopes were sent to her like running water.

While the circus was closing for the night,

tent entrances were being laced up and animals were sleeping back inside cages, he left The Monster Hall of Fame and walked to where he'd been watching her the whole time.

She was tired, biting her nails and waiting for the last minutes to pass.

It wasn't easy. He was still too much of a monster. He found himself trying to talk to her. He said, "Hello" two or three times before he realized he was actually speaking.

She put down a cup of bolts and broken glass and smiled at him. There were other people around the booth and suddenly he felt like running. But she wasn't leaving. She started to talk to him. Small things…she laughed about the weather…Maps were moving in her eyes when she talked.

More and more, he could see and feel. Even the Earth was spinning, a thousand miles per hour.

He looked at all the glass. "Doesn't it hurt to eat glass? Can't you hurt yourself?"

"No. There's a way to eat it so it doesn't cause pain. You have to know the secret."

"But you won't hurt yourself ever?"

"No," she smiled. "I'm careful." She turned the broken piece of bottle between her fingers. "There are worse things than swallowing fire, swords and glass." Her hands touched his. "What do you do for a job?"

"Right now I work at a factory. On the assembly line, I work. Riveting."

"See, now that's dangerous. I could never do that. I would never survive that."

"I'm used to what I have to do."

"So am I."

Later, she brought out a cake she had made and she passed him a piece on a plate with a glass of milk.

He told her, "This is the best cake and milk I ever had."

She smiled and watched him eat. "It's the only cake I've ever made. It's just from a box, you know."

She was doing things no one else had ever done.

He didn't even know he should be careful.

Blue sparks shot all around him as he cut through rusted metal. The sparks and slivers of steel just didn't hurt him, not even the fear of Dr. Frankenstein's blue lightning jars and his warning of fire. Now all he could think about at work was her. His heart was broadcasting images of her and he drove a rivet right through his hand, not even feeling that pain.

"It's an honor to work the line," his supervisor said. "There are plenty of people who would fight for this job. When I gave you this opportunity, I thought you could handle it. Look, no offence, but I'm going to have to let you go."

That was it.

He had a handkerchief wrapped around his palm. He didn't care what they said to him. He wasn't living in their world anymore. They couldn't hurt him. Someone was already being trained at his spot, trying hard to beat the clock, riveting, riveting, riveting.

It never even occurred to him that the circus would have to leave and she would have to leave with it. He never could have imagined something so terrible happening.

He looked at the sawdust left behind in the trampled field and for a long time waited for the bad dream to end so he could wake up again. He waited all day for her to reappear.

When the stars came out overhead and there were crickets calling around his feet, he lay down quietly on the ground.

Fire

In the morning, he left the circus grounds. How hard is it to fall into a dream—especially one you've been programmed for? He walked right into it.

On through the forest he found himself at the edge of a lake. Hours must have passed before someone's small hand touched his shoulder.

He turned around to see just a little girl. He wasn't speaking anymore, but she could tell how he was feeling. He looked like the wind had worn him down. She handed him some flowers she picked. His fingers were too big, they crushed the petals he tried to hold.

"You have to be careful." She showed him her game, tossing one into the slow current. It drifted gone as they watched, getting lost somewhere in reeds further on. She gave him another one. "Here….Just let it be on your hand." His hand was so big she could lay more and more flowers across it. "Now throw them in the water and you can make a wish."

So he threw flowers, thinking of someone as they went in, floated and sank. Circus music, cake and milk. He could only see her. The water cast back moving pictures of her as she was covering over with water and sinking, gone. He could only see her in everything that happened, where he failed and lost and kept losing. And then the flowers in the water weren't alone. With them was a little girl, dress floating around her, dragging her down and sinking. He thought it was just himself, falling in the water and drowning.

Moss grew on all the furniture with ivy going up the walls. His feet went deep into the green floor as he walked to the center of the room, stopped, sat down and then lay down.

Inside a soft wooden house abandoned in the woods, he looked up, out the holes in the ceiling. He could see the sky and tree branches moving in the wind while he started to fall asleep.

He had his last dream, moving, climbing into the heart of a tree, disappearing as voices made their way nearer. They spilled closer with their torchlight, dogs barking.

Dr. Frankenstein was looking for his monster too. He was searching all the sad places of the city where people forgot themselves. Cheap cold buildings, rooms with peeling paint and he looked into the faces on the street.

All he needed to do was perform the simple operation of taking the heart out and his monster could go on. It was such an obvious mistake on his part. He should have known it from the start.

At night a mob moved through the trees. The dogs were on leads and the men who held them had guns. They followed the monster's broken path through the woods. Their jumping light was bright across the sleeping dark green.

A man in the crowd was carrying the lifeless girl, still in drowned clothes.

When they found the monster in the house they threw the torches in. He didn't even move as the orange yellow rafters came down. The flames sent curling smoke into the stars.

He was able to smile, even with the fire, he wasn't here. He was far, far away. Where he was, the ground was soft sand underneath. He was standing in the middle of a stream, feeling the warmth of a sunny day.

There were trees and woods on either side of him and on the bank of the stream, she was there too. While he was entering this dream, he disappeared from another one, when the moss house collapsed onto him.

AFTERWORD

The Last Frankenstein was written after my return from New York City, about halfway through a long time of temp jobs and minimum wage work. Besides the sort of deadening world they created, I was also reeling from the death of a friend. One of the black and white movies we watched together was *The Incredible Shrinking Man*, which had a big effect on me, especially the scene where he meets the circus lady. A little later, I immersed myself in the legendary Universal Studios Frankenstein movie series: *Frankenstein, Bride of Franken-stein, Son of Frankenstein, The Ghost of Frankenstein, Frankenstein Meets the Wolfman, House of Frankenstein* and *House of Dracula*.

Though it's been years since I've seen those films, it was always great to witness the reappearance of Dr. Frankenstein's book under ruins, cobwebs, ice, or nearly burned. It was also good to know that however badly it ended for the monster, he would always be back. There never really was a last Frankenstein. Originally, I wrote this in poem form. I had all those same jobs too and wasn't far off from knowing what the monster felt. It must have all been real enough to write this for him.

February 10, 2014

Here in this enclave there are centuries
...the short and narrow stream
Of Life meanders into a thousand valleys
Of all that was, or might have been, or is to be.
The books, just leafed through, whisper endlessly...

—Randall Jarrell

PAPER GUIDE

where I wonder
twelve seconds
her own machine
thirty five gone
after falling twelve
the paper world
a pirate
only her smile
the rejects
instead of electricity
the buddha
learn from america
mild
the sound in a seashell
never mind
dream years
imagine a book
the reaction
before I wake up

outside, america was erasing its past
decoration day
buy densol
bookfiltration
leaving for america
voyage
up
the funeral of books
like a bird
a bird
the other
tickertape parade
a spell over every day
unwind
anything in a day
the heights
all the weight
blown out
her flags

A Bird
~~It was a whistle.~~

Of all things to find hanging from a ~~nail~~ ^{thorn} in the side of a chimney, it was a whistle. When Soro blew on it, as she had to do, it made a sound like ~~the~~ silk run through a ~~calliope~~ merry-go-round. That perfect tone was ~~still~~ breathing in her head when the sky started to flap. Looking up, she saw something bend in the gray clouds, then part through.

A stork the size of a person turned its white wings past her, looking at her ~~white~~ ^{with} the big green eyes of its triangle ~~that~~ face. Whenever its revolve came closest to her, the bird slowed and ~~spread~~ flattened its back and hovered in that moment as if to have her hop on. At last, fearing the dark plunge of the chimney more, she held on to its wings.

from original manuscript
reappears on pages 69-70

Where I Wonder

"This is where I wonder. Away from here, memories of my island home make a ship floating in a bottle. I was a librarian there. Every happy day when the children left in the afternoon, I put all the book colors back on the shelves so they formed rainbows again. It was those books that sent me to America. Myths, myths, myths. They told me stories. It took years but finally I followed. A long way from fairy tales, to here."

"Can't you get anything else?" Officer Doris blurted.

"Not really." The spool of tickertape flowed across the Library Commissioner's gloves onto the floor. "I can't understand a word." The machine continued to click with her thoughts. "What is that, some other language?"

"Aww! Forget it!" The librarian ripped the thread from the machine. "She won't make any sense. Wake her up."

Soro's eyes opened with a shock.

"You're clean, no problem with the check," her supervisor told her. "You can continue. There's a full pallet of books in the basement that have to be dumped."

Soro breathed and moved. "Thank you,"

she said. Gravity obeyed the stirs of her body as she became alive again.

She pushed her legs to the floor. The library world swirled like a broken compass, taking her several readings to know where she was. They had tested her. If she was fine, if the machine encountered no malicious thoughts, then she was allowed to return to her work.

Twelve Seconds

Twelve seconds of elevator time passed before the double doors opened at the basement level. Stacked in crooked shadows, tall rows of boxes filled the underground. The old fashioned lights that swung from the ceiling on cords had a life of their own, like lanterns in the breeze of a painting. And just across the room, making a bright orange smile in the wall, was the furnace.

On cold spring mornings like today, the library was warmed by burning books. A pipe above her shook with more books falling in. Chutes on every floor fed the fire. Beside the furnace, a wide shovel waited for the pallet of books. Already, the covers brightened with reflections of the flames.

Her Own Machine

Soro was back upstairs by noon. It took a few minutes to adjust to the electricity. The basement was a dark otherworld, another time, while the second floor was fluorescent with a hundred computer screens.

Her own machine was waiting for her. She pressed the switch and sky blue filled the screen. Then a tray opened. It waited for a book. A little arrow blinked impatiently.

The machine would read the book and file it among the circuits. She would wait for the light to shine. The book remains would be revealed and she would drop the rind into a trapdoor next to her desk. Tomorrow it would be waiting on a pallet to be burned.

The Complete Works of D.H Lawrence, Volume 3. So old…The gold lettering stood out from the red spine.

She wasn't supposed to think about it. They warned her not to. Books were only paper pages; the library was in charge of feeding all those words into machines. If anyone wanted to read, they could look into the infinite sea of electricity.

While the machine waited, it couldn't know,

it couldn't see what she did with the book.

Thirty Five Gone

At the end of the month, a graph would be computed to show how many books had been deleted so far. The Director of Central Library posted it on his door. In the short amount of time that was left of his life, he wanted to see his dream come true. The secretaries would stand beside his motorized wheelchair as he counted.

35, she wrote. The day's total for her. That would make a step in the climb of the graph.

"Soro?" Her supervisor stopped next to her desk. "How's the work going?"

Soro smiled. "It is good."

"Thirty five gone…" the woman read it as a matter of course. "There's another pallet of books downstairs for discard. Could you do it now? They're especially old though, could be dangerous. You better wear gloves." Her supervisor had her hands covered all the time.

"I will go."

After Falling Twelve

As usual, Soro counted the seconds in the elevator. But after falling twelve she was still counting. The fan churned, the lights spat like an oil lamp, something was wrong. She couldn't feel if the elevator was going down or in motion at all.

She let more seconds turn into a long minute before she pressed the button again. Then, with no change, she struck the alarm. A bell sounded feebly.

It wasn't unusual for people to get stuck in the elevator. Sometimes the mechanics of it got unglued. At least once a month it seemed to happen.

She slumped down against the wall to wait. She looked at her fingernails. She traced a path on the pattern of her skirt.

"Hello?" the speaker tube addressed her. "We'll have you going as soon as we can."

"Thank you," she said to nobody she could see.

So it was up to the silence in this place to pass by. Then she remembered what she could do. She was in a library! She laughed as she reached into her bag and took out the book to read.

The Paper World

She couldn't describe the feeling because so few knew it anymore. Everything was written on a page. She held the paper world. It let her unfold without the bright light of the present. She went back in time.

Halfway lost in story, the elevator gave a crunch and started to move. It took five more seconds down to stop and open rusted doors. By then she held the bag against her side as she hurried out.

The basement was dark but she knew where to go. A new pallet waited near the furnace glow.

"You will never know," she told it as she

approached. "You mistake all these books for meaningless."

The shovel was still warm and a flake of lost page fell off as Soro lifted it.

A motion caught in the corner of her eye.

Was someone there? The shadows hid everything. Sometimes it's just imagination making magic. A mysterious setting knows how you feel. She looked back at the stacked pallet and caught her breath.

The painted, engraved books were beautiful and ornate as palace decoration.

I have to hide them, she knew.

A Pirate

Like a pirate with a treasure to conceal, she found an aisle that led into boxes crowned by an inch of dust. She brushed off a carton and looked inside.

The box held a useless jumble of obsolete computer parts. They weren't like books when they age, these couldn't be read anymore. She checked another box to make sure they were all the same.

I can empty these into the furnace, Soro planned. I can hide books in the boxes instead. Nobody will ever know. For the next security check, I'll remember this in my own language. I'll save my English thoughts for their machine. I'll tell them what they want to know and somehow I'll get the books out of here.

Only Her Smile

She left the basement so tired only her smile kept her up. This time she avoided the elevator and took the stairs. It had been a long day. The last door revealed the library all cleared out and quiet for the night.

Every screen had blinked off. She followed the trail past them to her desk. The main switch had turned off her machine too. It would be hungry tomorrow. She couldn't believe what she had done. A pallet of books had been saved from the fire, a pallet of machine parts had burned in their place.

Scratching the mark in the column, Soro finished her work for the day. She put on her coat and stood up. The windows were dark. Many nights began early in the Alexandria library. Tall buildings grew shadows and smoke hid the sky overhead.

She heard the chain rattling shuffle of the cleanup crew coming through. She could see them down the carpeted aisle, brushing along… wearing prison stripes and pulling melon-sized iron weights on their feet as they swept.

The Rejects

Everyone in the trolley groaned. The lights blew out like candles.

The trolley had unsparked. This was the second time in a week. Its useless cable-arms shrugged in the wind apologetically.

Someone forced the doors open. A murmuring weary lot of passengers piled out. The night's coal rain shined on the tracks and the platform slanting towards the stairway.

Soro wrapped an orange silk around her face to fall in with the crowd. A long walk awaited her feet. Once she got to the street she would have to follow the pine colored lamps for miles, past apartments, stores, detours, barbed wires, finally into the Rejects, the ruins, her American home.

Instead of Electricity

It wasn't all like this. Some of the Rejects lived up to their name and people would be in fear of them, but further on the road she followed ended in lanterns, with candles held in trees. The Government sent her here when she came from the island. Like the rest, this was where she belonged. There was the sound of a different world from each yellowy house that she passed.

Soro lived next door to a man from the Amazon. Instead of electricity, he experimented with flying light. He crossed fireflies with butterflies. The garden around her little house would startle whenever they were about. From a distance, they welcomed her, painting themselves in the air.

The Buddha

As she went up to her door, more blurs of color scattered past her from the ends of curled flowers, like fireworks off and on and gone. Soro opened her house, struck the match next to a candle and let it show her the way to the center of the room. There, she knelt beside the statue of the Buddha.

"Thank you," she said, "for bringing me back."

With the lantern lit, the room suddenly began again. She recognized shelves of rescued books. The library had been good to her—what they thought should be burned into ash, was instead finding her.

Whenever she placed a new book before the statue, it felt like saying a special prayer. Soro set it beside the dancing candle flame.

Learn from America

In the morning, Soro was tired as she stood in line for interrogation. When it came her turn, she slumped down into the seat and seemed to fall asleep.

"My name is Soro. I came here in exchange from my island. We still teach from books there, but I will learn from America the better way. The library will show me."

Mild

After the usual waking confusion, Soro stood. She had passed the test.

"You may return to your work station," the machine told her. Lights popped like a movie marquee towards the Exit. The electricity skipped a few burned out bulbs.

"You may return to your work station," the

machine repeated. By the third request, it was programmed to give her a mild shock.

Soro walked along the flickering row and opened the plastic soundproof door.

The Sound in a Seashell

She stopped. There was no sound of work… As she waited, listening, the silence was loud as the sound in a seashell, a heavy opened ocean roar. The carpet crushed out the pad of her footsteps. There weren't any computer chatters or fans or voices calling around. Entering the library coliseum, she realized she was all alone.

The big clock wasn't lying, the day had only begun and everyone should be here.

"Hello?" Soro said.

She turned around and pressed on to the Administration office. If something strange was going on, they would know.

The electric secretary wobbled its thick lenses towards her. "Identify yourself."

"My name is Soro. I work in the Preservation Department."

Following a long series of clicks and whirs, the secretary spoke again. "You should not be in the building at this time. The library is contaminated."

"I don't understand?"

"Book presence levels are unacceptable for human contact. You must leave immediately. This is not a drill." The front door was triggered. It slid open to a gush of warm sunny air.

Never Mind

Never mind the tedium of work all day, she was outside; it was spring and the birds were strung in every green tree. After the dull colored warehouses ended at the curb, the park began across the street. It was a kind of miracle that lived every day in the midst of the city.

Pretending the jet white scratches in the sky were actually cloud fingers pointing to show her the way, she answered, "Okay, I'll go into the trees." She took off her shoes to walk on the grass.

Someone gardening a long time ago had planted oaks and maples, firs and cedars, in the bowl that naturally formed at the foot of the hill. Whoever it was, she thanked them.

The grass got thicker and mixed with wildflowers and she was soon wading deep. Once, she could have sworn she saw a deer, but how could that be?

Dream Years

The leaves made an overlapping wall to hold out most of the city noise. What was left could have been the sound of distant ocean surf. She thought of the dream years when this is what all America was like.

Her back to the tree, she saw how it must have been. Animals came here too. A blue jay and a crow appeared. There went a squirrel along a branch. If she had the chance to hide all day, she believed she really would see a deer make the slow walk into the rocky stream below.

Soro opened her bag and held the wrapped sandwich. A windmill in the Rejects ground the flour for the bakery in back of the blackberry plot. Tomatoes and lettuce filled in the taste.

Beautiful thoughts carried her to a vision where there were factories turning out gardens like this. She thought of them shipped and planted everywhere, like something in a book. She checked her bag and remembered all her books were safe at home. Nothing else to read, she pretended, opening her hands to look at the printed lines on her palms.

The Reaction

When she closed her hands and looked back at the park, it had changed. It was the reaction of imagining a book.

A wooden sign had appeared with the word: Library.

"Oh!" she said as she read it, startled and sat up. Nothing in this land had prepared her to find the thing she had always looked for.

A path led her to where another sign was planted. A painted arrow pointed through the ferns, deeper into trees. Library. Not far away, she could see its shape in the leaves, she could feel its pull.

Before I Wake Up

The Library was built with tall marble stems like a temple. Rows of windows glowed. Stepping stones walked her right to the stairs, guarded by lions on either side. Their golden eyes watched her. A tail moved, a paw crossed, but they let her pass.

"Thank you," she told them before continuing. Taking hold of the polished brass handle, she opened the door.

Not even inside yet, she nearly cried at the sight. "This can't be happening. I must be asleep. Really I'm under the tree with my eyes closed. But before I wake up, I will live in this dream."

Outside, America Was Erasing Its Past

In the time between two worlds, not knowing how long it would last, she stepped onto a marble floor. Big rooms opened on either side, filled with books. Her breath was rushed. Polished oak card catalogues stood in the middle of the mirage.

She ran to one and pulled the drawer. Directions to books were typed on ivory cards, pinned like butterflies inside. Outside, America was erasing its past. It went by so quickly.

Someone laughed warmly nearby.

Soro whirled. "Hello?"

"You found the Library," he slowly said.

"It's okay to be surprised," he said. "Anyone who makes it here is. I remember I felt the same way. Don't worry though, this is real." He gave her a book to feel.

The illusion was disappearing. She was holding a book.

He laughed to comfort her. "This is the Real Library. Only people looking for books appear here." He pointed, "Look. In that room is Philosophy, Science and Religion, and over there is the Music collection. You can hear them."

She could see the ornate cabinets of Victrolas spinning 78s. A gypsy love song found her ears—a hundred years old—and it was still preserved, floating in the air.

"You might like to wander, just to know that you are here. There's more upstairs, and also below."

"So many books," she marveled.

"And the books you saved from the furnace were delivered last night. There's a gold plate with your name on a shelf over there. Only a friend of the Library receives that award."

Buy Densol

Back on the Alexandria trolley, advertisement images flickered above the windows…*Buy Densol for the Perfect Look!* The city went by, filled the glass, shot along the rooftops, seeming to never end. Soro glimpsed people caught on the street, billboards, wedged in buildings, smoking vents. To ease the procession of mile after mile, stop and go, she thought about the Library. Was it real?

Bookfiltration

Narrow memory-tree limbs curtained the doorway with an arc of programmed branch tangles and cardboard leaves. Soro said hello and the door tracked open.

The Secretary was too busy to notice her enter the Central Library. Soro went down the hall, into the computer dawn. A few people veered from side to side. It was still early, there were coffeemaker steaming factories.

A web of office partitions led to her little cube. The walls had holograms built to suit her taste.

The machine blinked at her, "Good morning. Proceed with Bookfiltration."

Leaving for America

When Soro touched the switch on her desk, the walls of her work-cube became a scene from her island. It was all around her. Imagining she was there, she could think better. She heard water. She remembered the old face of a woman there, telling her about the place she was leaving for, America. "It feeds on your dreams," she had been warned. "If you are not careful, your thoughts get confused." Soro knew those words to be true. As long as she kept herself strong she could carry herself through.

Voyage

Even though the cart next to her was jammed with condemned books waiting for her, Soro went to the elevator. The metal door opened and she stepped inside, on her own for the voyage to the basement.

"The books you saved were delivered last night." Did someone really tell her that?

The usual gloomy view greeted her when the elevator opened. The jack-o'-lantern grin of the furnace and frozen lengths of boxes faded into the back of the room.

She whistled. The echo carried everywhere. It was a pharaoh's tomb, covered in dust.

The boxes she hid yesterday were gone. Carried away, footprints made marks in the sand leading to the metal hatch of the book furnace.

Up

The furnace was always warm. She listened to the heavy deep presence of the fire. Pushing the big gray hatch open, the chute dropped into the sound of burning orange.

Whenever she got this close to the end, she held her breath. There was no sign of the books. The only way to save them through here was by going up the chimney.

The Funeral of Books

Soro was in the flow of smoke and hot burning words, climbing the chimney rungs laddered into the bricks. Tilting her head up, she could see a distant round eye of daylight looking back at her.

A chute opened somewhere below her and another pour of books flapped like bats.

She hurried on in the funeral of books, climbing for that light at the end, to catch her and raise her out.

Like a Bird

When she emerged from the chimney top, Soro sat on the edge like a bird. Her clothes were crow black. Soot and little burnt feathers of paper stuck all over her. She coughed. The library smokestack sent out strange dead sentences. Smoke signals. She could see the dark snow drifting over the city roofs.

"But where did the books go from here?" she wondered. "Someone takes them up all this way and then what? Do they set them on a cloud?"

The railroad yards clanged with a change of cars. Traffic bent loud on the roads, but nobody passing by saw her in the heights.

Some explosion below her made her look into the chimney. A flower of bright orange sparks. By the dying light it made, she discovered the hidden item hooked next to her dangling foot.

A Bird

Of all things to find hanging from a peg inside the chimney—it was a whistle. When Soro blew it, as she felt she had to do, it made a sound like silk run through a merry-go-round. That perfect tone was still breathing in her head when the sky started to flap. Something big bent in the gray clouds then parted through.

A huge stork turned its white wings past her as it circled the smokestack. She saw the big green eyes set in its triangular face. Each time around it came close to her, slowed and flattened its back and hovered in that moment, to have her hop on board.

What choice did she have?

Soro finally took a chance and joined its wings.

"You found us again," the Librarian said. They stood together on the marble roof of the Real Library.

"Is this how you bring books to the Library?" she asked.

"It's one of the ways."

They watched the crane unfurl its wings and sail back into the forest air.

"Would you like to go downstairs?"

"Yes," she said. "It helps me to see this place. I wish I could be here every day."

"For now, it's good to have you on the other side," he said. "We need people of the other world to believe in us. You know, we're waiting for our chance to come back."

"What will it take?"

"Something will happen," he said. "It will be soon, I think."

They went down the stairway to an oak door, to a hallway leading to the reading room. Soro took a step into the painting. Other people sat quietly at tables or hovered near shelves.

Tickertape Parade

Everyone marched into a big steel room and sat in rows. An electric clock hammered on the wall saluting nine o'clock then the Director was wheeled in. An attendant plugged him into the wall socket while someone else attached his wires to the machine. Every month he addressed them, he seemed less there. *He?* Soro looked confused. Every month it got harder to tell where machine began and ended.

"Progress report," he said and the attendants backed off. A tickertape chattered. "Redefine and activate the pressure release limits of each committee and identify ways the system can be proactive."

Soro twisted against it. She couldn't listen to the words, they didn't mean anything to her. She remembered her own language and she spoke it in her mind until the Director's speech was nothing but the nighttime buzz of jungle bugs.

A Spell Over Every Day

A butterfly landed on her hand and glowed. The firefly luminescence poured in its stained glass colors. She wondered…Was it right to change any living creature—even something already beautiful, into something different? Or was everything altered by America? A spell was put down over every day, wasn't it? When the butterfly light went out, she waited for it to return. Sometimes they short circuited, but it would come back on in a while.

Unwind

The Rejects were resting. It was late, just the unwinding of crickets and a candlelight in Soro's window. She was still awake. She watched the Buddha shadow on the wall. All she knew was she belonged in the Real Library in the woods. How could she continue with the city job when there was the beauty of a magic place waiting? The shadow remained content as long as the candlewick didn't flicker. "In the morning," she decided and lay back on the bed. The blankets went over her like a tired warm sea.

The wooden clock woke her up with an abalone bell. The world of sleep was gone, but she remembered the dream long enough to smile as she reached out of the covers to touch the alarm.

A long time ago the old woman on the island told her, "If you can tame and control your dreams, you will be able to do anything in your day."

Soro decided, "Today at the library, a wonder will happen."

The Heights

Soro slid the box lids aside and saw the row of glittering letters on the spines. An entire encyclopedia set from the 1930s. Inside were pictures of the world they lived in and the complete knowledge of their time. They had reached the heights in their steam powered age.

She pushed all the books into the two bags she wore over her back like a pair of heavy wings, then she went up the chimney.

Every little shape on the street below crept between the building columns and signs. People were the same dots going back and forth. "I don't have to be like them anymore," she said. She let the books lean on the bricks and she reached for the whistle. Taking a deep breath, she gave it sound.

Just like before, the graceful bird came down obediently, once around the chimney then again. Catching her and all those books, the crane sunk like a lead fishing weight.

Blown Out

Soro and the crane went at the earth fast and missed. They crashed in the silver satellite dish that sent messages to space. That instant cut all the blue screens of Alexandria, everything at once, as the light of the Central Library was blown out.

Her Flags

The wind and rain shook the shacks and trees of the Rejects. Storm forced everyone inside. It was already known something happened in the city; people had been talking about it since last night.

The windows of her room let in the breeze like everywhere else, only she wasn't there to see the curtains blow and laugh like flags around her books.

My History of Libraries

Many moons ago, growing up in Seattle, our closest library was actually a little house in the neighborhood. Every couple weeks, when it was a nice day, we would walk there, past Food Giant and Fuji's Five and Dime, and go down that long street full of wooden or brick houses, gardens and lawns. The library house was just off the sidewalk, up some cement steps, or a chase up the sloping grass. Inside, the rooms were all ordered by subject. My sister and I and our neighbors if they came along would hurry to the Children's Room. I used to get a lot of books on dinosaurs and airplanes and any adventure stories that looked good. Then we would walk home holding them and I was looking forward to running upstairs and ly-ing on the green carpet in that spot of sun to read. My grade schools always had libraries in them, and every week or so our class would go to check out books. There was a time in high school, when I was in the library with a bunch of friends. It was before class and we were talking and laughing. The librarian came over to our table and told us to hush. My response was borrowed from someone I idolized at that time, my best impression of Jack Benny saying, "Well!" Later on I worked in a beautiful college library. One of my jobs was to restock the big wooden card catalog. Sometimes I would even make fake cards and sneak them in. I remember doing that for a short story I wrote, filing it by author, title and subject. By the end of schooling, I had decided to be a writer and I got the idea that the way to do this was to take on as many different jobs as possible, in other words to experience the big world of America. So I became a parking lot attendant for a while. I went to New York City and worked in a glass factory, did filing and envelope stuffing. From my job in a skyscraper, I could look out the window way up in the air and see the little cars and taxis and people. Then I came back West and worked in restaurants, washing dishes. Of course I met all kinds of people and wrote so many stories. But by the time *Paper Guide* was written, I was back working in a library. I was just married with a baby on the way. A lot had changed in libraries while I was gone. Computers were taking over. I became friends with

Dennis who used to run the Mendery until the board decided that department was no longer needed. Books would soon be a thing of the past! The library was pushing for a glorious all-computerized future. One of my jobs there was sorting through books to be discarded. They actually did have a big chute in the wall. There was a dumpster in the alley. Once I climbed inside and tore some color plates out of an old dictionary. Pictures of butterflies and ocean animals. Soon after, when we moved to Ohio, I got a job in a public library. It was an amazing historical Carnegie library in an old rail stop town. I wrote my novel *Ohio Trio* on my lunch breaks, sometimes wandering the streets to draw pictures. The library had a beautiful fireplace room where old farmers would sit and read the paper. I could see where the card catalog used to be, but now it was a circle of computers. People would come in and ask how to find books. After school, children would arrive to play computer games. When we returned to the West, I got my first fulltime employment in a university library. I liked the circulation desk and all the characters I met. I had a great job with Eric in the Mendery as he taught me how to repair books. It was a real thrill to take a beaten-up book and after some surgery put it back on the shelf, healed. We would laugh and tell stories and listen to books on tape while we worked. Stephen King's *Gunslinger* series, *1984*, *A Confederacy of Dunces* and many more. But that time in there was short. As I had seen happen before, the library administration shut the Mendery doors, deciding that books and their upkeep were not important. Even now, there is serious talk about moving the books out of the library and storing them "off site." This will open up all kinds of room for computers. At this point, it does seem like dark times for libraries and I do go looking for that Real Library in the woods.

January 18, 2014

S
T   B
A   E   S
R   C   A   W
S   O   N   H   T
        M   D   E   H   L
        E   N   E   A
                                Y   N
                                        D

Part One
Stars in the Last Frontier

Part Two
The Sand Rivers

O

STARS IN THE LAST FRONTIER

She saw herself, brought back in time and trying vainly to convince people where the future was taking them. Why would anyone believe her? Who would listen to a girl telling them the truth? She would just end up watching history repeat itself, like a film she'd seen before.

So this is how it is, she thought at the end. America has eaten itself like the snake looped around with its tail in its mouth. "We came from Earth and went to Earth," she said. This last night that was filled with hundreds of stars and the circling light of a returning rocket. Before morning it would be landing in the desert somewhere, less than a year since it left. What did they find on the moon, did they learn anything at all? From over the ocean, she watched it curve on to the horizon, until it blinked out of sight.

When she opened the time machine door— just for a moment—she only wanted to see what it was like inside—but it was already too late. She slipped through time, back to America.

O

It was cold on top of three hundred stories, even though she wore layers of clothes and curved in a sleeping bag under a shelter. The chill of the wind would get through.

A small fire burned an orange glow that was the only light.

Shivering, she reached over and put another piece of broken furniture on the slow burn. Sparks snapped as fire took hold. Living on the roof, the rest of the world seemed a planet's distance away. She was alone on a mountaintop with no one to answer her thoughts.

Just like when she left Alaska to begin with, she said, "If I can get out of here and this situation, if I can only find somewhere I belong."

As she fell asleep in the wind on top of the skyscraper, where she had been and the things she had done became a part of her dreams.

With a scratch and a click, the record player next to her picked up its arm and the black vinyl spun again. June Carter warned her about chasing a wandering star, when nobody knows where you are. Her song floated and swept over the ledge.

She turned with the dream that took her thoughts back to Alaska, where her journey started.

O

Blue with stars, the state flag flapped over her in the icy wind. The 21st century hadn't changed much about Alaska where she was born. Anchorage was still the same cold dark nights it had always been. She was caught in something that wouldn't change.

Running through crooked alleys in the freezing, towards the lights of clubs blasting music that drifted and piled like snowbanks onto the white cement, it felt like escape was just around the corner. Even when she wasn't looking at the stars, she felt herself floating unconnected and millions of miles away.

It got to the point where she was waiting for something to change so badly she was hoping for luck from horoscopes in the newspaper.

Every day, she found the newspaper and read her fortune.

Then, after months of trying to gather her thoughts, all the pieces revolving around her began to fit, taking the only form possible: there was a truck in the parking lot and the highway leading out was on the other side of the hill.

It was cold that night as she got into the truck. He's going to hate me for this, she knew, but it's the only way I can be happy. She turned the key and took the Alaska Highway south. She kept driving through into daylight when she finally stopped and fell asleep in the parking lot of a big restaurant, Hobo's Korner Kitchen. The glassy walls and the bright neon sign of the place woke her up in the evening and she started driving again.

For days, the road and other cars were all she looked at. Watching down the hood at the passing, darting yellow lines on the road was meditation. It was the time of the year when there were purple flowers starting to grow on hills beside the road, with hundreds of miles to think while she drove. Mechanized farms were patched on either side of her. Black electrical wires unspooled for hours.

Everything was only time—to know if she was right or wrong—to find if she should have done things differently. "I'm on my way to someplace new." That's what she told herself, over and over and eventually Alaska was gone.

She was traveling through Canada towards the rest of America and she could read the blue road signs, "America 514 miles...America 165 miles..." She was getting closer all the time.

Every time she stopped to remember, there were people and things that she would miss. Everything had to be left behind her, sold off into stores, dropped off in boxes, forgotten.

But she had to bring her record player and LPs. Her music was the sunken treasure from another century.

It was easy to lose patience with the radio stations and the signals from America. All day she went through them, from one end of the dial to the other, searching. It was hard to drive without good music and rain started to fall again while more signs of American civilization began to appear. Cars, clusters of fast-food restaurants, condominiums, shopping malls, walls and reactors; they took control of the landscape.

She actually welcomed them, as if she was

emerging from her own Dark Ages. She had never been to the lower states. It was her idea of civilization: she wanted to be where something new was always happening.

As the city neared, it looked like more clouds on the horizon…the heavy gray blue smog.

Seattle had turned into a place of wet freeways and cement. Green ivy growing from the rain held clinging to dark buildings. Her red pickup truck soon got lost as she clogged in with rush-hour traffic.

She kept her eyes on the Space Needle, fixed like a rocket in the middle of skyscrapers and humming power stations. Slow moving in her window, it was still a science fiction tower, a tall strange flower dipped and rooted in cement and left for a hundred years. But she liked the way it looked. This could be the last remaining totem pole out of all the wooden thousands carved along Puget Sound.

The window wipers weren't moving, they had been stuck halfway across the glass since somewhere near Ketchikan and now the rain warped her view. She had been in such a hurry, she never stopped long enough to have them repaired. Hitting the dashboard or windscreen wasn't any good either, but she kept hoping that was what would wake them and make them move again. Alternating between gas pedal and brake, she crept along with the stalling traffic.

The going was so slow across ten lanes, she reached across the seat and put a record on. Johnny Cash and June Carter were breezing into Jackson.

This century didn't make records. They had been discarded like pottery. They were left for her to uncover in the ruins or in rotting ghost town stores. This favorite record had grooves like tree rings, fifty years old. As it played, she rolled down the window so the rest of the world could hear the scratch of music.

While she was glued to the rest of the cars, the rain still smudging her view, an explosion made her jump in surprise. She blinked as the Space Needle fell down in a cloud. Old buildings were going down all the time now to make way for new construction jobs. Time and the weight of things were making them fall. Through its ghost they'd be putting up something else.

In this city, Alaska seemed much further away than a thousand miles; it was another planet.

She wondered if she made a mistake, if this

city was where she was meant to be. Moving off the freeway, she parked on a steep hill. There were all sorts of things to consider about staying in this city, but the truck made it easy for her. When she left to get a cup of coffee, it decided for her.

As she walked to the top of the hill and happened to look over her shoulder, she had her last glimpse of her pickup below.

It drove itself, backwards missing cars, a red blur that became airborne off a pier and splashed into the deep. She had been warned about the emergency brake, but she never had to worry about it before.

Now the truck was underwater.

A small crowd pointed at the rising bubbles and waves. Traffic stopped along the waterfront. She pushed her hands through her dark hair and held a scream inside. Her hands fell and rested on her hips while she took a deep breath and exhaled slowly…A model of perfect self-control. Everything has a reason. This is meant to be, she told herself, this is fate telling me not to move anymore. Disasters have to be taken in stride.

But it wasn't that easy. Sirens went through her and past her and she cried with her hand pressed against her lips. Police cars were already cordoning off the area down below and a helicopter was on the way, dropping to circle the water. The eleven o'clock news would eat it up.

"Okay Carla," she told herself and wiped her eyes with the back of her hand. She turned around and held her hands tightly, "It's okay. It's nothing but a truck underwater now." She thought about fish on its upholstery, seaweed and barnacles growing on the metal eventually.

Walking to the coffee shop, she wanted anything else to think about. Now that she was here, she couldn't leave.

Her reflection crossed windows and she looked up at the skyline being built like the sides of a box all around. She tried not to start crying again.

She noticed the sidewalk trees didn't have leaves. They were like skeletons.

The door of Loch Ness Coffee swung open for her.

In a week or so, I'll be out of money, then what will I do? I have to get a job and a place to stay.

A loud silver machine steamed out a cupful and she paid and found a seat. Sliding up against the wall, she sat down and pulled a newspaper off the bench. Glancing at the headlines—the big news was the rocket searching for life in outer space—she poured a small bag of sugar into the drink. On the sugar packaging was a picture of the Space Needle.

When she read *The Last Frontier*, she read it again. All she could think of was that Alaska license plate which had those same words. Whenever she thought of that phrase, it had to be something attached in letters to a car.

She unfolded the newspaper and looked at the advertisement photo of a parking lot filled with used cars for sale. A man in a white cowboy hat, Gary Justice, promised in big black letters, "Every car is a star at The Last Frontier!"

Why do they keep pushing cars? She thought about that. Listen Gary, I know you want lots of money, but can't you see what you're doing to the planet?

That was stupid, but it led her back to the truck she didn't have any more. What's going to happen now? She sighed as she stirred her coffee.

She went through possibilities. Will they want to fish the truck out? Probably. Hopefully the water's too deep, polluted with so much junk already they won't bother. But what if they do? They'll want to track down the owner. They'll find out it's stolen. Then they'll find out about me…She stopped stirring and watched the current she had made. The steam that rose from it disappeared. Then what? I'll have police after me…Wanted for drowning a stolen truck. Wonderful…

At least the coffee tasted good.

The best thing she could do was wait it out, she decided and she returned her attention to the newspaper folded open next to her. "The Last Frontier." She wondered if that cowboy and his used cars knew about Alaska.

Gary Justice was selling the best and largest selection of used cars in Seattle. He was on billboards and car bumper stickers and advertisements in magazines, on TV and radio and he even paid people to hand out his brochures on the streets.

O

There wasn't a job she could like, it was either working tables or working at a desk. "What possibilities," she sighed, "but what can I do? I have to survive. I'm just working so I can pay rent." Otherwise she would spend her life searching the country for records. She would like that, taking to the air in a flying machine, going from town to town.

9 to 5 and home to eat and sleep could have convinced her this was all a bad dream. Factories owned all of America; they left their mark on everything on the land. It looked like the machines took over and made people a part of their metal.

She was worried about the robot way everyone had to live. The buses unloaded everyone every work day, amid the noise of construction and the thick smog curled through the air.

It would only be temporary, she knew her life would get better, so she answered the phone for minimum wage, "Hello, this is Carla, can I help you?"

Outside the window of the office where she worked, it was an eighty foot leap through grit to the crowded street below. Cars and cabs inched along. Buses carried the words *The Last Frontier Is Here*.

O

From her window Carla watched ships crowded on the water, moving synthetic oil, coal, and the factory products from all over the world. They formed long waiting lines obscured in the haze, then they docked, unloaded and left with the last of Washington's forests. People went to museums for the memory of trees, where things that used to be were kept like photographs.

She wondered what they were pouring into the sea, and why. The salmon water was dark and oily, and in places fires burned on the surface. Volcanoes surrounded them, she could have been in the land of dinosaurs.

People were given warning notice by the newscasters on TV if the breathing levels were too dangerous. Yesterday, everybody was advised to stay indoors for the next few days while fires burned uncontrollably and smokestacks gushed pitch black. "Don't worry!" the weatherman predicted happily, a storm was expected soon. It would blow all the bad air away. In the meantime, everyone was advised to stay indoors.

It got worse, but the good news was she couldn't go to work. Staying at home, she listened to scratchy records, while flying aircleaner machines plowed outside her window, inhaling through the sky trying to filter clean paths above the city.

The curtains were pulled so she didn't have to see them and the blues music was turned up loud enough to drown out the machinery. She turned the record sleeve over in her hands.

O

It came from a place nearby, wrapped with barbed wire to keep people out. Her favorite thing to do was to explore those forbidden places. She would find ways through the fences and sneak through what used to be, where the years were left like abandoned streets.

It would take her all day looking through the rubble, searching ancient buildings for artifacts of interest from the last century. Here's where all the old parts that fell out of the city landed in layers like geology. All of America was here.

Most of the twentieth century ended up buried in there, on the dangerous floors covered in broken glass and hypodermic needles, with a snow coating of wall plaster.

Somewhere in the maze of broken rooms, collapsed ceilings and walls, she would be lucky and find her treasure. Records were the fossils she was really after. She played them on her portable record player.

O

The fire illuminated the small shelter she had built for herself. The sun was still shoved underneath the east.

She was glad the police had forced her to hide. It may not be the best hiding place, but she was far above the confusion that was taking over down below. Living on a roof had been peaceful compared to what she escaped. That's what her nightmares were all about.

The record player next to her was recharging while she slept.

Boxes and cans of food were stacked against the walls. She found meals and everything she needed to put together this small house in the miles of rooms and the halls below.

At first, she thought she could live in a storage closet or a locked room. Nobody had been to work in days but the risk of being caught seemed too great for that.

It was safest on the roof. No one would think of looking up where rainbows were formed in the steam and water vapor. She didn't intend on staying too much longer anyway, just until she could make a new plan, until things calmed down.

O

At first she thought they wanted her for the sunken pickup. It was her fault, but the stolen truck had gone to sea weeks ago. Kelp should have grown around her guilty fingerprints by now.

When she came outside of her apartment onto the street, the two of them surrounded her, police badges mounted on their helmets, along with the names of their sponsors, The Last Frontier and Double Cola, stitched to their bullet-proof vests.

"What did I do? What's going on?"

"You're a runaway, aren't you?" the officer asked. He held her arm tightly, but he wasn't hurting her yet. Who knows where she might have ended up if there wasn't an explosion?

A bomb went off down the block. The black cloud piled out over the street and in that moment of distraction, she broke free.

It didn't matter if they shot at her. She ran.

Along the pavement, into the cloud, the

piles of rubble and destruction. She tried to lose herself, dodging through, jumping over wrecks of metal, newspapers, bottles and all the remains.

She slipped through a wall, escaped to the other side, back onto the crowded street and rushed with that river until she doubled around to her apartment building. It was dangerous to return, but there were things she needed for a life on the run. She couldn't leave her music behind; that was what kept her going.

No police at the door. She went inside and ran up the stairs.

The hallway looked empty, only the sounds of a crying baby, a science fiction movie on someone's TV, and overhead, the buzzing, dying light from the neon tubes hanging along the ceiling.

It took her a few minutes to gather everything. She quickly put on different clothes in case the police were still looking for her and she pushed her hair up underneath a hat.

There were places all over the city she could go to hide, but she didn't want to live on the street, she had seen what that did to people. The first thing she said as she stared at all the buildings around her was, "Up."

Her running and hiding took her into the sky.

O

Daylight glowed in the seams of her shelter. For a week, the roof had been clouded in a haze and now the warm sun wagged in the flapping cloth entrance, waking her up. She yawned and rolled onto her side. For a minute she just lay there and counted shadows and held the patch of sun in her hand.

Finally, she crawled out of the sleeping bag and pushed the curtain aside. The sunlight made her blink. She stood up outside and stretched. It was warm enough to take off one of the sweaters she wore.

Blue sky spread overhead and she walked to the edge. The smog had fallen halfway down the glass sides. Overnight, that much of the pollution had disappeared and now she could clearly see all the buildings around her. The mountain ranges stood out on the horizons.

It was such a beautiful day she returned to her shed and got the record player. She carried it over to the ledge where the drop off was three hundred stories and set it down carefully.

The needle bit into the spinning vinyl crackling before music began. Breakfast came in small pieces out of a box and she combed her hair over her shoulder while she ate.

She had changed her idea of civilization since living on the roof of a skyscraper, having enough time to think about it all. She was learning more all the time. Everyone's needs are very simple. If we could start over, we would not have to take as much or make so much either. America would have to be different. But all you had to do was look around and the worry occurred, Maybe the world is being destroyed because of what people are doing...

This was just the way life had become by the 21st century. She had grown up in this—all her life, she was waiting for it to happen. It meant always being on the edge of terror. It took some getting used to; it took a lot of strength for her to go on. There were people who couldn't make it; she had seen them in the ghost towns. They were broken down, just like machines. They stared at the sky and they tried to hold themselves to the ground.

Just looking around her, seeing what had been done to the beautiful world, she felt rare as a moonbeam. She could get away from so many things, turn off feelings inside her, shut down the things that made her human, stay far away from the ground, up on a skyscraper roof, but she was alone. She wished she could be with someone she liked; she missed what it was like to hold someone.

Tonight she hoped there would be clear sky—that constellations, planets, galaxies and all the stars in between would shine on her for the first time in forever.

When she finished breakfast, she listened to more records. The sun rolled overhead and she examined the other buildings for signs of life. It would be nice to see someone else out there, but nothing moved behind all their shining windows. Above the layer of pollution, there was only her and a few straying birds.

She hadn't been to every floor, but she was making a map of the skyscraper underneath her: where the food was, where the water was, where she could take a shower. This was one of the world's tallest buildings, but she had noticed something strange. Many of the floors in the middle of the building were scaled so small they couldn't be used at all, they were like dollhouse floors. There might have been hundreds of stories stacked like drawers in the stairwell behind a door. She could run her hand across the miniature carpet. Tiny office furniture. It was frightening to see. She didn't know what they were for and there was nobody to ask.

On the 279th floor, she collected an armful of packaged sandwiches from the vending machine and she broke into the beverage machine for some Double Colas.

She saw her reflection, holding a crowbar and stolen meals. Is this what she had become? Maybe it was time to say goodbye to skyscrapers and clouds, and go back to see the ground. She went to the elevator to gather her things from the roof.

The elevator doors opened with a Muzak fanfare and she pressed the button for the 300th floor. It sung her up there.

When she got out, it was a short walk down the hall to a tile pushed away in the ceiling. Crawling through, she balanced along a girder to a hatch above that led onto the roof. When she came out into the warm nighttime breeze, the air was clean and clear as a mountain peak, stars in the sky, to be breathed in deeply.

She collected her records and a suitcase from her shelter. The Milky Way glowed like a river and she appreciated one last slow look from the corner of the roof.

The sound of wind wrapped the smooth glass sides, rattling the antenna spires, and the full moon shined its electricity on the empty buildings. The streets were hidden by pollution. It was a risk to go to that place under the clouds, but that was where the other people were.

Like a growl from those depths, the startling roar of engines rose over the building behind her.

A huge aircleaner bobbed in the draft at the edge. Magnetic docking lines discharged, anchoring the machine to the building, pulling it in closer. The fans hummed, keeping it steady in the breeze. Red lights blinked along its sides in dots and a searchlight flashed and cut its beam in her direction.

Someone had caught on to where she was. They must have spotted her shelter from the air.

For a moment she was frozen by the sight, then she was awake, running a for the roof hatch.

Would they be waiting to arrest her if she went to the streets below? By the time she reached the elevator, she knew. She couldn't leave the building. There were plenty of abandoned floors. She had to hide somewhere new.

O

The elevator door slid shut and her ears popped with the fast descent. Still, it would take a long time for the three hundred stories to flash away as she fell through floors. Muzak still played inside the elevator, like some musical cockroach that could survive anything.

Floor number 21 lit up green and there was a long five seconds until the doors sighed and began to open.

Carla went into a quiet deserted hallway.

The elevator shut behind her.

Gray smoke splashed against the windows, moving like something alive. This was where the layer of cloud had fallen. It couldn't push through the glass, but it wanted to. When it shifted, coiled for a moment, she caught a glimpse of the streets below. A blistering mirage of a world. The smoke gave her that vision, then it hid it again.

A dry voice called to her—she wasn't

alone—someone was collapsed against the wall, behind a chair. It was a man, but he was disappearing. His breath was leaving and he was turning into sand. His feet and legs were spilling away from him.

"I was so close..." It was his voice she barely heard, so softly now as his words left him. "I tried to get away..." He held out a hand, but his fingers were disintegrating, turning into gray dust in his coat sleeve and he had to let his arms fall. "I was..." he whispered and even his words became sand in his mouth. He was nothing but sand in a suit.

It all happened so fast, it was like a horror movie, and she panicked. The only thing she could do was hide herself again.

When she passed an office, she crashed opened the door.

The room had space for a desk, two chairs, and a filing cabinet. She tripped over a plastic bucket around the corner of the desk, knocking out paper and a Double-Diet Cola can. There was space enough to hide lying down. "I never should have left the roof. It's still too soon." If the morning ever came, she could look for life. Curled behind the office desk, she shut her eyes.

To keep the world spinning even though it seemed to be falling apart, she dreamed meaning into what was happening. In the morning she would go to the ground floor and it would be peaceful, after the storm, as she walked outside with the plants already taking over. She was surrounded by the New World. The Last Frontier was made for her. She could move through it and do anything she wanted.

O

She woke up surprised to be under a desk.

Electricity had ended during the night. Only a pale light in the glass panel of the office showed her that day had come. She found a different way back to the elevator. She didn't want to see the dust remains of that man.

At the end of the hallway, near the elevator doors, a tall window showed on the wall.

Against the glass with the morning sun falling through, she looked out to the streets below. The clouds were gone. Things were desolate and still as an empty photograph, or a black and white movie after Martians conquered Earth. Complete silence in the still down there. The sun was bright and warm—she could feel it on her palm—the sky blue, but the city seemed to have ended. Life may have just blown away.

When she realized the elevator couldn't work, she had to use the stairway to get to the first floor. Waterfall echoes bounced along the cement walls and the stairs.

Dizzy with that sound, she kept thinking of what it would be like to finally open the door at the end. Would she be Dorothy in Oz? After all those floors when she unlocked the exit door, she stepped out among all that was left behind, the debris of their last day on Earth, the tipped and broken things. There was no sign of the people or their ashes, though at any second she expected their invisible presence to become real. The floor of the lobby crunched with broken glass.

Smoke blew in through the breaks, wisped and carried the sound of the wind inside...She pushed a door open and a newspaper caught around her shoe. In the shelter of the doorway she bent down and pulled the newspaper up, but the words and pictures were blurred.

The walls of all the buildings were darkened from the polluting cloud. She stood there waiting to at least hear a distant explosion rattle, wondering what to do next. Even though the city looked very empty, she couldn't be sure. It wasn't like she dreamed, it was so very silent, a silence more than any dream. No city could ever be this quiet.

She felt conspicuous walking in the street. The buildings went clear up into the blue sky, all around her, and she could imagine what they would become. Green towers with a hundred years of ivy. That was a long time from now, disappearing in a blink.

Cars with opened doors, going nowhere.

The entire city had become a ghost town; everywhere there had once been people, the wide streets and stores and companies, empty.

Alongside her were all the places where people used to be.

She entered the crashed open door next to her. There were faucet handles in the first row, all kinds of useless electrical appliances shelved in unlit aisles and a pyramid stack of paint cans.

Just to see what it would be like, she found the cash register and took out the money. Nothing happened. Nobody stopped her. It didn't mean anything. The cameras weren't working, there was no one to care.

Outside, she let all the money fall from her

hands onto the cement. The dollars drifted away down the sidewalk, like they had blown off trees. She left it to float along the curbs, doorways and alleys, falling in with all the rest of the blowing garbage.

O

After an hour of walking in this photograph stillness, she thought it would be a relief to see a conquering Martian or a beleaguered National Guard retreating in tanks, but nothing waited in the long shadows or perched behind broken glass.

Only a few blocks away, was that same steep street the truck rolled down to sea. So what? Every car left along the curb was parked forever.

She stopped at the little Peace Park, a narrow triangle of grass, leaves, shrubs and a couple small trees. The statue of a girl was wrapped with origami birds. The stones on the path came from Hiroshima, Japan. Now they were at home with the pieces of Seattle. Water pouring from a gray rock fountain made a running stream, creating pools along the curb. Carla leaned down and felt the clear water.

That peace was snapped when she heard a noise in the debris. Something small, approaching, moving through the trash.

Opening her eyes, she saw a duck, a green necked mallard stepping orange webbed feet around a crushed can. He walked with a purpose that led him towards her.

Carla felt sure that she was seeing things... The first sign of life!

She dried off her hands on her jeans.

The bird walked past her, up the pavement hill in a wavering line.

Carla followed at a careful distance, worried she might disturb him and cause him to fly away. But the bird seemed unconcerned with her and maybe unable to fly, went on regardless.

Uphill, climbing to Capitol Hill, five more ducks and geese joined in, forming a single file that was added to every few blocks as another bird would appear out of somewhere. A rusty singing sound gathered in waves and moved in the branches, from street signs to the roofs of cars, small flying birds. Far above, circled at different heights, seagulls turned and pigeons roosted along ledges of buildings.

Life is gathering itself, she thought. We're coming together. The city was still alive, it had just changed. But she kept looking for people... she couldn't accept the idea that she had to be the last person. Not after everything she had gone through.

The duck led twenty three birds and her past The Last Frontier used car lot. A billboard of Gary Justice waved across the backs of the broken, rusting cars.

The birds didn't seem to tire like her, carrying her suitcase and records. She counted fifty birds in front of her now, including a white goose with orange eyes.

Nearing the top of Capitol Hill, she could finally see where they were all marching to.

Cut into the cement and shining with sunlight—a water reservoir, big as a lake.

Birds dotted the sky and she could hear the sounds of more.

"I'm so glad to see you!"

The words stopped Carla cold.

The greeting came from a duck on the curb.

"What?" Carla's voice could have escaped from an Egyptian tomb. She coughed and stared in amazement at the duck. It's been so long since I've talked with someone, she realized, I'm imagining birds can speak. "Are you—?" Then she noticed the blink of metal, a microphone hidden in the feathers.

"I was so worried! It looked like there was no one left." The voice was being transmitted through a speaker, it wasn't a talking duck. Someone had rigged it to watch for her.

That meant that the planet still had human life! She was struck by the lightning of that feeling. She wasn't the only survivor!

Carla asked "Who are you?"

"You'll be seeing me soon enough. I'm over here, where the birds are taking you. I would have met you down there, but I'm not good at going down hills. My brakes aren't what they used to be."

There were too many trees in Volunteer Park for her to see where he could be. The ridge was like a small forest with the only remain of man a heaped wreck of a car.

She wondered if there could be someone inside the car. Maybe he's watching me with a telescope and talking to me with a radio?

She asked the duck, "Are you in that car?"

"You could say that," the duck answered.

The junk car was barely a square from her distance, but she could see it wasn't a car, the shape was wrong. It looked more like a car kneeling, if that was possible. Then it stood up. She could see even from far away that it was shaped like a person. It clanked slowly in the grass towards her.

"Is that you?"

A robot, making the ground shake and sending birds airborne away from it.

She had never trusted robots—the fear that shot through her made her tense. I know I can outrun him, she paused. He was crushing a new path in the brush. Of all the people left in America, and it's a robot!

He told her, "No, don't worry! This is just my suit. This isn't me. Sorry, this is the best I could do in the time I had." That thought made him stop. He was closer, but his voice still came through the duck, "How did you survive?"

"What do you mean?" It took her a moment to answer. How was she supposed to know? "What happened around here?"

His voice took a moment too. "I guess there's a lot we have to talk about."

"Yes..." Then she had to smile, "Like why am I talking to a duck?"

The duck laughed with static. "Once we get closer, we can speak directly. It was just easier to microphone a duck and send it off like a note in a bottle. It saved me the trouble of walking around, searching the whole city for life. It's not that easy to walk attached to a car."

"Yeah, I believe it." She took a step towards him, "Well..." she leaned towards the duck, "My name is Carla, by the way."

As if it had enough, the duck raised its wings again and took off. She didn't know if her message had been carried with it.

"I'm Dodge."

She heard his metal voice come from a distance. "Dodge?" she whispered.

Dodge slowly moved his arm and waved to her and she waved back.

Walking towards each other, she was becoming aware that he was as much car as person. It looked as if a car had been pulled out like a blanket and wrapped around a human form. Metal letters across his rusted chest spelled out his name.

There may have been a dark blur behind the glass of the headlights, but there was nothing really human in the face.

She stopped before him. "So you're a person inside of all that?"

"Yes, of course. This is the protective suit

that allowed me to survive when the sky fell. I'm fireproof, airtight, air conditioned, fully operational." He motioned himself like a car salesman. "I know what it looks like—I look like a tin can—but it works. That was my main concern. But how did you survive, Carla? How can you still breathe?"

"I don't know. I just came down from that skyscraper," she pointed over her back, "and everyone was gone. Did everyone turn into sand and blow away?" She stared at the figure of car parts for an answer. Then she added quietly, "Maybe I'm just not seeing them. Maybe they're hiding."

The words sat inside of him, turning like something in a ticking clock. "No, I'm sorry Carla. They're gone."

Her eyes followed a pair of long blue cranes soaring past him, over the lawn towards the museum. The sun shined in pieces on the green water of the reservoir. Lawns spread out behind Dodge, with trees and all the birds sitting, flying or walking around the white marble shape of the Seattle Art Museum. Further off, a dinosaur's back of stretching glass greenhouse. On her right was a tall brick water tower surrounded and overgrown with ivy. Pipes ran from it. In front of her, the metal carperson put his chrome hands together.

"I'm still trying to piece it together," Dodge said, "All I know is guesses...I think it was a plague the way it hit like a wave and took every person away. Something was in the air we breathed. It came in as a cloud, but it wasn't like the normal smog in the city, this was deadly poisonous. But nobody knew. It happened so fast and strong wind carried it everywhere. As far as I know, across the world. People disappeared. It's like the Black Plague in the Middle Ages."

And suddenly she saw him as a knight, a man from that far away time, standing before her, rusting in all that car armor. "Yes, it is."

More birds were landing. He wore their reflections in his metal. He changed the subject and pointed to a sofa in the shade under a fir tree. A comfortable relic from the old America she had known. "You look like you're tired after that walk, Carla."

"Yes," she nodded and she thought, Why not, Carla? This is a strange sort of robot, but he seems nice.

He offered to take her suitcase, hooking it with a finger and easily carrying it across the grass.

"Thanks."

He set it down next to her when she sat on the cushions.

"I brought this furniture from one of the mansions over there." He pointed at the row of white houses, balconies and columns all over-growing with plants. "When I first saw you headed this way, I thought you would like this."

"Well thanks, Dodge, it's very comfort-able." She kicked out her legs into the lawn and leaned back with her arms crossed. She couldn't help closing her eyes.

"You can sleep if you're tired," his voice buzzed.

"I'd like to know more about you. How did you know to get in that car?"

"Honestly, I was told to build it."

She opened her eyes and stared at him. *"Told?"*

"I was warned that everyone would vanish."

"Vanish? That's impossible."

He was hissing, the car metal was almost steaming as he fumed on it. "It is possible! Just look around you, you can see that it's true."

"It doesn't mean everyone is gone though. I'm still here."

Carla could see steam coming out the vents in the side of his head.

As far as she could tell, there were only two survivors, and she still couldn't be sure he wasn't a robot.

Dodge sat down on the grass and became a steel box again.

He had to let the steam escape and the hot plates on him cool. "I know, Carla...I never thought everyone would be gone, but I built this protective suit. I had to."

"Who told you to?"

"Someone, something I've never seen before. I hope it's okay to tell you. It was like an angel came to me, or sometimes it looked like a girl with wings. It's hard to say exactly, but she warned me what to do. I could tell it was more than a dream. I believed her." His voice was calm again.

"So I started building this suit out of the nearest metal I could find. An old car. I shaped it into my body. After all that work, I created this air-proof armor. I finished just in time too, just before the storm broke."

"You're a regular Noah, aren't you Dodge?" She tapped his metal.

"No. All I could do was save myself. I guess

nobody would have believed me anyway." He sighed. "That must have been when you were up on the top of the skyscraper?"

The hill looked down over the silent city. Birds flew in the air, drifting.

She was watching the sky above the tall buildings, "I was living up there and I saw the clouds falling like water going down, but... how could? Why didn't people just leave? Why didn't they run, they could have hid like I did."

"They didn't know," he said. "We were used to the clouds. Weren't you? Then the whole sky just came down so fast, it got inside of everyone before they could do anything."

Carla said, "I had dreams I never thought would come true. Somehow I knew this was going to happen too. And last night, I dreamed all of this before it happened. I could still be in that dream, couldn't I? This is all too strange to believe."

"I know," he said, "Maybe your eyes have turned into crystal balls. It looks like the same world, but it's not. Tell me something else you can see, that you know is true."

She thought for a moment then smiled, "If I tell you the sky is green, you'd believe it?"

"Through these headlights, it does look

green. Is it still blue?" He sounded worried.

Carla stroked her chin, squinting one eye up at the clear sky. "You can't tell?" She took her time with a smile, turning her glance back to him.

"No, I can't tell. It's like looking through sunglasses."

"Well..." she wandered her gaze back upwards, wondering on her response. If I tell him the sky is green, she thought, he'll either think I'm lying, or he'll think he's on Neptune, or worse. Then he'll never leave that suit. But if I tell him it's blue, she decided, he'll be relieved he's still on Earth and things can return to normal.

She said, "Even though you're dressed like an astronaut, Dodge, the sky is still blue. The air is fresh and it's a beautiful day. Look, there are whales floating around out there in the ocean. There's no sign of pollution, or bombs or plagues anywhere. It's just peaceful life."

Quiet.

"You could take that suit off, Dodge."

"I don't know," he paused, "I want to, but there's still a chance that poison remains somewhere...It may be coiled up in the very last breath of that factory stack over there on

Queen Ann Hill. As long as the possibility exists of the smallest dust of pollution surviving, this is my only protection. It keeps me alive."

She looked around at all the trees beginning to flower, the ocean and mountains and she spoke into the clean air, "Well, it looks fine to me." She breathed in deeply. She stared into his headlight eyes, "You've got to know that this can't hurt you. I don't want to turn into sand either, Dodge. But I would rather take my chances here than live on top of a skyscraper for the rest of my life." Or inside of a car, she almost added.

O

"What were you like when you were a person?" Carla asked that evening, "I mean, before you took cover inside all that car metal. I bet you were really shy." She was draping dandelions over his metal shoulders, ringing them around him.

"I've never been good around people," Dodge said. "I loved animals though, I used to have cats. This whole city used to be filled with cats. I guess they couldn't live through the poison. Only the birds could fly above it. Now I like birds."

"But what about girls? You could leave that car suit and be with me..." she knocked on his metal chest and smiled. "I've been imagining what you were like, when there were people around. I think I have an idea. You were probably a lot the same, only I think you hid yourself behind something other than car parts. You probably stayed inside most of the time. You must have gone to your job, some office thing, or a lab or something. And at the end of 9 to 5, you escaped back home to your apartment where you lived alone, except for your cats."

"Thanks so much, Carla," Dodge said. "You've really painted a picture of me."

She laughed, "I didn't mean that in a bad way, I just figure you became an afraid person. It's okay, I was too! I think we are so much alike. I was happy in my room, listening to records. I've done a lot of running away in my life. When I finally escaped to the top of the skyscraper, it was because I was at the end of my rope. All I wanted to do was get completely away from every last person on Earth. I felt like I really didn't belong here at all. I used to wonder if I was brought here as an experiment to test what life was like on this planet." She laughed and touched the rusting steel over his arm, "I completely failed though! I didn't fit in at all. I tried to get as far away as I could. A skyscraper roof was as far as I could go! But after a few weeks of being alone up there, I needed to go back down and guess what? All the people were gone!" She put a last flower on him. "Maybe we don't need anyone else, do we Dodge?"

He was quietly listening to her, dented with the dandelion flowers. "We're lucky we found each other, Carla."

"I'm going to sleep out here with you, Dodge," she smiled. "You won't fall over on me during the night, will you?" She rapped his steel. "Do you sleep lying down, Dodge?"

"No. I don't really sleep anymore. There are things that keep me awake."

She lay back on the sofa.

"Tell me a story, Dodge."

"Oh..." he stared up at the sky.

"So I can fall asleep," she yawned.

"Alright, I'll make one up." The stars turned overhead, millions of miles away and there was a rocket out there somewhere too.

"There was a planet that was all covered in trees. That was all they had, trees. No rocks, no iron or steel or plastic or glass like we have, they had to make everything they needed out of wood. But they weren't foolish about it, when they cut down a tree, they replanted two or three. It worked fine for them, their houses, and cars, and airplanes and boats and everything was made from the trees."

"What about records?" she sat up on her elbow and her dark hair went over her shoulder. "Were there wooden records?"

"Of course. They were made from the diameter of a tree, bigger trees made longer playing records and small ones were 45 singles."

"Good," she rested back down, pulling a blanket over her. "Everything came from the trees..."

"Yes, they even had wooden telescopes. That's how they looked through space to see our planet, Earth. They watched things we had here. They were especially interested in the metal. They imagined all the ways they could transform their planet if they had metal like Earth did."

"Why weren't they happy with wood? I like

wood. You should have a wooden suit, Dodge," Carla said sleepily.

"They really wanted Earth metal, so they built a rocket spaceship. They were so pleased to have a way to get that metal, they had a big celebration when the rocket left into space."

"How many people were on the rocket?" she asked.

"Two," Dodge said.

"A man and a woman?" Carla was waking up.

"Sure, a man and a woman."

"Interesting..." her eyes glittered up to him.

"Anyway, they watched their green planet get smaller and the gray and blue planet Earth got bigger. They passed satellites made by our planet. They were so excited, they almost grabbed them and went home, but their mission was to go to the planet and make some kind of trading deal. They hoped to be able to do everything our people had done. Soon, Earth filled up their wooden portholes and they were caught in its orbit. They went into the atmosphere and burned up like a match. Nothing was left of them and their wooden spaceship."

"That's a terrible story, Dodge!" Carla sat

up again. "How could you tell me that story?" She grabbed a drooping flower and threw it at him, "You're not a good bedtime storyteller at all!"

"Well...It's not over yet, Carla," he said.

"Yeah, sure! The moral is, because of their deaths, the people on the wood planet decided never to go into space again, looking for things they didn't have, or didn't need to survive."

"Well, right, but that's not all. When the spaceship burned up, it scattered the tree seeds that they were bringing to trade for metal. The seeds fell down over the surface of our planet and quickly took root and grew. This was a total blessing for us, because there were so few trees left on Earth."

"Good," Carla said, laying back down next to him.

"But that's still not the end of the story, Carla."

She rolled over on her side and looked up at him, "Hmmm?"

"The people from the wooden planet didn't know that their trees were actually stronger than our metal. When the trees grew on Earth, they were indestructible. There was no way to cut them down. They grew into huge forests and jungles."

"A happy ending!" she laughed.

"Yes," he answered. "Now you can have sweet dreams."

"Well..." she rolled over. "I don't really understand why their spaceship burned up in the atmosphere if their wood was indestructible... But I won't question it, if it ruins a happy ending."

"Ahhh..." Dodge mumbled and looked back at the moon.

O

It was upsetting to her, that he wouldn't leave his carsuit and she wasn't getting anything but arguments from him about it.

"You don't get it. I'm a magnet to any last pollution. For instance, do you know what the half-life of nuclear waste is? Thousands of years!"

"But look at me, I'm here, I'm alive!"

"Maybe you're immune. I don't know."

"You've got to live like a person while you're here, Dodge. There are all kinds of dangers to living, anything could happen. What if you got hit by a meteor?" She whirled and tossed a softball sized yellow flower at him, "It's all a risk, that's life! But it's not all bad. There are good things worth taking a risk for."

She touched the spot where the flower hit. "I know what it's like. You're just afraid. You have to open up to it." She had to keep him human.

All the birds on the water took off so suddenly that she lost her breath for a second. She saw a pair of flamingos go by, a pelican and some kind of a stork, turning like a mobile in flight down the hill.

"I have been taking readings and gathering information," he explained. "When I'm content with my assessment, I'll emerge."

She stared at him. "See that's what I'm talking about! What do you mean? You really are beginning to sound like a robot. I bet every day you spend in that thing, it turns you more into a machine. Please, I need you."

But he had become quiet, like a car.

Leaving Dodge to his computations, she went back across the street, up the steps into her mansion. She slammed the door. She needed to calm down.

Though there was no need to keep track

of time anymore, she still needed it. She had been living on Capitol Hill for a week now, in a mansion near the park. She chose it because she liked the gray stone Chinese lions that roared silently at the street.

Past the lions, the walkway led winding up to the front doors. The house was so big she hadn't explored it completely. There might be sliding panels or tunnels through walls to other rooms. Treasure could be hidden, heirlooms and pirate doubloons, useless now, but beautiful colored, shining gold.

Everything was different with America gone.

For once, there was no need to be worried about getting food. When she was hungry, the greenhouses were full of growing food and there were hundreds of grocery store oases when she wanted something else, like chocolate maybe. Candy lasted forever.

Shelter was wherever she wanted to be.

She and Dodge would laugh and make bonfires with money and she was decorating the park with diamond jewelry, hanging strings of pearls in the trees. A ruby watched from the eye of one of the lions flanking the walkway.

Last week she had Dodge pull a shiny piano

into the middle of the tall grass, to become a lawn ornament. Portraits from the museum made good scarecrows for the gardens.

"Hopeless!" she slammed the door behind her. Did he want to be a robot? Who would want that? Sometimes he could be so aggravating. But she thought about him all the time… he was always on her mind.

He couldn't follow her inside the house; his weight would crash him through the floorboards and trap him down in the coal cellar like a Civil War train.

She was always alone with her thoughts in here. This was the house of sound. It was so quiet, she could hear ice melting from the freezer, dripping to the basement, making a cavern eventually.

Ancient pharaoh faces were painted inside gold frames at intervals along the wall. They watched history around them. When she arrived, they watched her move into an upstairs room. She was surrounded by a curving half-moon of glass, shining like Mission Control TV screens.

Down the hallway, she went through another carved doorway and she was in a greenhouse. Tropical birds and butterflies flew around the green corners.

It was like another atmosphere, or walking underwater, thick steam and moisture. Plants scratched around her. Trees were planted in a circle around a black pool of water. She sat on the brick edge. A goldfish surfaced near a lotus flower.

The steamy vapor was thick as fog, winding around everything. Sound could be felt: frogs and crickets, the stream, the drum of dripping water, birds, wings, and the slow swirl of the ceiling fans.

She shut her eyes...

She thought of Dodge. He surprised her with a bicyclebird and all the music to ride it. That was out of the blue. "He must be thinking as much about me too."

He told her, "In all this day to day quiet I've been able to put some of that technology we used to have to a good use. We will soon have all the electricity we need. Of course..." he put a hand to his imaginary beard philosophically (a gesture he had copied from her), "The birds won't like my windmills, but they'll adjust."

She pictured huge spinning sunflowers making electricity. She smiled, "Be careful. Windmills look like flowers. They might attract giant hummingbirds and bees."

"Yes, that's the way it works," he said, enjoying her thought. "They will gather the pollen and scatter it over the whole valley." He pictured the gardens, "Windmills will grow everywhere and we can harvest them for electricity."

"And the big bees will make nests in the mansions and fill the floors, wall to wall, with honeycombs. We can mine them. We can sneak in the basement windows at night when they're asleep." That idea was too good to be true, but she had hopes. She still thought the 21st century could be magical after all. "What else should we make?" she asked, smiling.

He laughed, "I've already made you something. Bring your record player and a record and I'll show you."

"What is it?" Her eyes were eager and lighting up.

"A surprise, a surprise, you'll see, hurry."

Dodge watched her rush off towards the house, looking over her shoulder before she went inside. Then he clanked over to a tree stump. It was leveled smooth as a table, with wires for roots. Carla is going to like this, he smiled under all the car metal.

When she returned, he set the player down for her and plugged in a wire. "Now," he said, "let there be sound."

The needle dropped into a scratchy groove. A gypsy guitar filled the air, through two hundred speakers on trees all around the park.

The sound sent up clouds of startled birds.

But that wasn't all, there was more. He was really starting to surprise her, but I shouldn't tell him, she thought. Or should I? She was more confused about this than anything else.

She could handle the disappearance of America compared to falling in love with a car.

"I made something else for you," Dodge pointed towards the sofa out in the tall growing lawn. Next to it was an object draped with blue sheets.

"Dodge, you didn't have to do that."

"Well...Wait till you see what it is! You've never seen one of these before! It's...well, I hope you like it."

They walked over and he extended his arms above the drape like a magician about to expose the next wonder of the world. "Here you go!"

He flung off the cover and laughed at her surprise, at the electric way her face lit up.

She was speechless...Not because it was a

bicycle, but because it had huge white feathered wings attached to the pedals. Her hands were around her mouth and she whispered through her fingers, "I can't believe it." Her eyes looked into his headlights, "Does it work?"

"I don't know if it can fly. Maybe. I kind of forgot about gravity when I made it. It might be more of an ostrichcycle, but it will look good, I bet. The wings flap when you ride it."

"It's so beautiful," she went around it slowly, taking it in as she circled, like the unwinding of Amelia Earhart.

"Try it, try it! See how the wings move!" He loved it all. "You can fly the Pacific, I bet."

She put her hands to the handlebars and sat on the seat, starting to turn the pedals with her feet. The machine was perfectly balanced, the big swan wings lifted and waved as she pedaled.

It pulled against the ground, and Carla was a little scared that it might really take off. She slowed down—maybe the ground wasn't a bad place for this machine to be. It doesn't need to fly.

O

"There's a rocket on the Moon!" the

radio-sized voice of Dodge floated on the air.

She thought she couldn't have heard him right, that somehow his words had changed in flight to her. Getting to her feet, she went over to a window.

Outside in the park, Dodge was holding a strange copper feathered antenna, pointing it at the blue sky and reading numbers from a counter.

The noise as she opened the window caused him to turn to look at her.

"I'll be out in a minute," she called. She shut the window and went to meet him. What was he looking at? What was happening on the moon?

There were probably rivers on the moon, oceans filled with sand.

She started to laugh, but turned it carefully into a smile instead; she didn't want to hurt his feelings. Her shoes squeaked when she walked on the bricked greenhouse floor.

Across planes of sunlight, Ottoman carpet, oak floor, she squeaked around the marble staircase that grew like a corkscrew.

Dodge was waiting for her outside.

He was turned like Mt. Palomar to the pale moon. "Why would they go to the moon?

There's nothing to see but dust. It's no different than here."

"That's not true. We still have trees and birds, water and life."

"But will they find people up there? It's an awful empty world without people."

She was about to agree, when suddenly his car head swiveled like radar to the left. "I'm getting a radio signal, Carla!" Dodge pointed at another spot in the clouds. An aircleaner was approaching, not far away, buzzing their way fast.

Carla looked for a place to hide. "How does it know where we are?"

Dodge was surprised she was scared. He was steaming with excitement. Inside him, he was listening to the incoming message, "It's okay, Carla. Don't worry, it's another survivor like us!"

"But we don't need anyone else, Dodge!"

The machine was filling the sky. Then its engines cut and it drifted in to them silently.

She groaned. The sound of the engines became loud in the air again and the gust raged at the trees and fields on the top of the hill. Carla held her hair back from her eyes, flashing dark around her face.

The airship shadow crept towards them.

"Where's it going to land?!" She ducked as it swooped.

The airship sailed overhead, went past, towards the three tall red and white radio towers. Canons shot grappling cables out and anchored the big ship in between the three points. The lines tugged and stopped the machine, metal creaked and strained and the propellers whirled to a stop.

It was quiet, the silver flying machine hung in the middle of towers, webbing itself inside with a triangle of anchor wires.

"Are you sure this is okay?" she asked, because everything was so quiet now. She remembered being chased off the roof of the building. While they neared the huge spider web, the time passed and there was still no sign of the pilot. "I'm scared, Dodge," she held the handle on his arm.

"Don't worry, it's another person. It's incredible luck. There are more people out there!"

A minute passed and Carla said, "Are you sure that you weren't talking to a recording or something, there's no sign of a person up there."

"Some of them are automated, but I

definitely talked to a person. I'm sure of it." He stared up at the whale like shape that was harpooned in between the radio towers. The wind made it seem alive.

But as she looked at Dodge, Carla heard a noise above.

A hatch swung open in the side and a tiny figure up there waved, shouting something. A moment later, a rope ladder began to lower itself, falling to the ground when they had stepped safely away.

To pass the long time as the pilot climbed down, Dodge tried to determine the rate of descent. It was a simple mathematical equation and he soon had it figured. Distance, speed, time. He spent the next minute making more whirring observations, equations, while they waited nervously.

The pilot wasn't a man. They both realized that. A woman called, "I knew there had to be more people around! I knew I'd find you!"

But it was her turn for surprise when she let go of the ladder and turned around to meet them.

A girl and a car.

She pushed her fingers through her short brown hair and collected herself. She was a bit taller than the girl and older by ten years or so. And who was the companion, a walking car? In another moment, her blue eyes showed that she understood the most important thing. At least she wasn't alone.

"Hello, I'm Dodge! I talked to you last night." He extended a hand of rusted car parts and her hand didn't quite wrap round the metal grip. He couldn't feel the warmth in her hold. He continued, "This is Carla over here."

She stepped over a pace and smiled, "Hi Carla. My name is Joan. You're the first people I've met." When Joan looked at Dodge again, there was still a little doubt in her eyes.

O

They were talking about America, about what used to be America.

There were hundreds of candles for light, as Joan paced back and forth browsing along the catwalk in the library.

Dodge asked her, "How were you able to survive, Joan? I still have to wear this suit." He was leaning in through the window from out-side, with his metal elbows on the ledge.

Joan found a book on flying machines. It was filled with balloons and creaky looking bi-planes that must have flown as slow as floating in the last century. "I was lucky to be in the aircleaner when it all started happening. The cloud layer covered the entire land as far as I could see from above. The radio warned me something terrible was going on. I just stayed in the air for as long as I could." She flipped a page and there was a drawing of a man with strange wings attached to him.

"That cloud turned all the people into sand," Dodge said.

Carla was sitting at a table with a cup of tea, watching Joan.

Her shadow moved along all the books. "The cloud seemed to drain back into the ground. I monitored the radio until there were no voices."

Carla said, "What was the cloud?"

"I don't know," Joan said and Dodge nodded with her. "But it's gone now. If it was something alive, or a curse, it seems to have done its job. We have to feel lucky we're still alive. So far I haven't found anyone else. Even the dust of them has disappeared."

She knew he would be awake

O

It was sometime early before dawn when Carla woke in her mansion room. She dreamed America had been rolled up like a carpet and taken away.

Morning was far and she didn't want to wake Joan just to talk about her nightmare.

They had been spared (Carla and Joan had escaped above the clouds, while Dodge hid inside armor) but Carla wondered what they were supposed to do now. We don't know how to remake what civilization has done.

Listening to the night, and all the sound caused by the moon, Carla stared out the windows and decided to go talk to Dodge. She knew he would be awake.

She wrapped a blanket over her shoulders and padded through the house shadows, downstairs and outside.

Dodge was standing under a tree not far away. Did he ever sleep? Did he watch the moon all night? He noticed her walking up to him; the long grass swishing around her bare legs and her white blanket glowing in the dark.

"I can't sleep," she said. "All I can think about is what happened."

He nodded, "Me too..." watching the sky, the shadows that covered the moon.

"Can't you stop watching the sky, Dodge?"

An owl went by and dropped down after a field mouse. The bird flapped up out of the grass with it caught in its claws, flying back to a nest somewhere.

"I don't know what we're supposed to do." She didn't want to watch the moon with its shadows. She looked at her hand; she looked at the cold city buildings; she looked at the tire tread shoes that Dodge wore…Anything but the empty moon.

Her eyes went back and forth across the park and darkness.

On nights like this, it seemed as if ghosts were in the grass, hiding, while the wind blew up fog from the sea.

Bats were flying out of the museum arches.

She saw the reflection of stars in his metal armor.

Dodge said, "Joan wants to search for more survivors using the aircleaner." He pointed at the sleeping machine. "We could go with her, Carla. We could scout and remap the country, just like pioneers, starting everything all over again."

She looked at the place where his words were coming out, a slatted space with a gas mask grill and she nodded. "As long as we're together, Dodge."

"It will be fun to go on an adventure. I've been sending out radio messages all night, telling the world we're on the way."

The faint clicking of Morse-code whirred out of him.

"Well, keep trying. I'm going to go get some sleep," she yawned. "I might be getting tired again."

He was deep in silent things, head tilted toward the moon. Moths batted against him and he didn't notice her drift away.

O

Sometime during the last ice-age, valleys and rivers had been carved through the Northwest. Rocks were shaped or crushed and carried for miles to other places and dropped. Years stuck under all that ice. Then the glaciers moved off and left the land to the rain and ocean. Life started again.

Water dripped off the steep roof edges and a

cool wind blew the drapes, carrying the sound of engines.

Carla woke up, turned and looked out the windows at the rain coming down in a green slant through the leaves.

The engine sound stopped. Joan was awake early, testing the flying machine, preparing for their expedition. It was a good idea to make sure everything was in perfect working condition before they set out, but Carla worried for a moment that Joan might be leaving without them.

Outside was all the sounds of rain.

She got out of the warm bed and dressed.

Dodge was waiting for her, sheltered a little under a tree. His suit was running orange from the water, rusting.

Carla wore two sweaters with a green slick raincoat.

She noticed the metals of everything man-made disintegrating, but she thought, for some reason, it couldn't affect him. He still refused to get out of the armor, he still pointed at the uncertain sky. The car would have to melt off of him with time.

"Dodge, what's happening?" she gave him an umbrella smile.

"Good morning, Carla." He walked into the rain to her. "Joan says we should be ready to leave in an hour or so. We're going to explore the four corners of the Earth!" He flourished a rusty arm, as if he was a knight riding off. But once he moved, he seemed to be frozen with rust. "Aww, I have to start oiling these car parts," he groaned.

"Just like the Tin Man," Carla said, thinking of Oz.

Steam blew out of a hose on that arm made of old Detroit steel. The smoke snaked in the rain and wind, over his shoulder. It took a few moments for his arm to fall.

She walked along with him slowly. His steps were heavy and creaking. It was like walking with a very old man.

They went past tree branches dripping pearl necklaces and diamonds. The airship hung in the extinct radio towers. One day the towers would fall. They would make long triangle fossils in the clay.

It seemed like an hour to get to the zeppelin, Dodge complaining and wishing he had rust-proofed himself.

It was crazy to be in Seattle and forget about the rain.

Suspended like a gray dripping cloud, Joan's airship waited for them.

Dodge seemed to hit every puddle and stream. The ground turned into mud underneath his weight and every step he was dying battleship steel, sinking deeper. "It seems like the rain follows me," Dodge said.

The rain fell over both of them. The wet on her skin shined. "I like the rain," Carla gave him a smile.

"I even dream about the rain," he wheezed.

"Me too," she said. "Last night I had a really strange dream. If you want, I can tell you."

He steamed along next to her, his feet left lakes in the mud, but his voice was warm, "I will always listen to you, Carla." Some other kind of light was in the headlights.

"Thanks. That's good to know." She crossed her arms. It was a little cold out. "I was standing in a very large teepee. It was bright inside and there were two dead bodies laid out on the ground. I was nervous, I didn't know what was happening but they showed me. The chief sat on the other side of the teepee and he told me what to do. He said to wrap the bodies in white bear skins and place the bodies in the bottom of the river.

"It's wintertime and the water is cold but perfectly clear. I can feel what it's like to be at the bottom of the river. He said in the spring, the bodies will move downstream and everything will be alright. I can remember what he said to me too, 'Dead spirits don't bleed.'"

She looked back at him and laughed and said, "It seemed to make sense in the dream, but I don't know exactly what it means now. Still, I feel that it was some kind of a sign or something."

She watched Dodge and asked, "What do you think?" She could only imagine what he was like inside. "Hmmm?"

Dodge was quiet, thoughtful and then, from the metal that made his voice sound like train travel, he said, "I'm smiling. I think that's a good sign for you...I think it means that you can put aside something that ends."

The propellers of the aircleaner were turning. Carla and Dodge were directly underneath the airship. Joan was waiting for them. It was a long way up.

Carla made a groaning noise. Dodge was silent, maybe calculating. Carla put her hands on the rope ladder.

As she left the ground, he said, " Carla,

I can't go with you."

She turned a look to see him stuck to the earth.

He stood there like a castle attached to the ground and continued, "I won't be able to join you. I can't climb that ladder. The ropes can't hold me."

He looked sad through all the metal, "But I could stay here. I can monitor your travel. I can take care of the birds. I can try to find more people...We'll still be close, Carla."

Carla was ten feet off the ground, her hair was wet around her shoulders and face and she blinked from the rain. "You've got to come with us, Dodge! We can't leave you behind. I'm not going to lose you, Dodge. Just leave that car and follow me."

She descended as he raised his hands, un-latching steam from the hinged locked pan-els on his sides. He was opening, unscrewing his helmet into the rain slowly as a submarine hatch.

She picked up an umbrella to cover him.

"Carla, if..." his voice rusted quietly next to her, "If you don't like me when I climb out of this, I will understand."

"Don't worry, I do."

The Dodge parts came off and she saw his face, features, only for a mirage second, a dream blink, after he took the car metal off, as he turned into dust. The suit filled with sand.

It happened so fast, his disappearance was just a second. There was nothing she could say. She let the umbrella fall.

The metal trunk of him was standing there. The rain was filling the hollow shell and the trickling dust was all that remained of him.

O

The rain continued for two full days and nights while Carla sat in a chair next to the window. Joan made her food, it was the only way Carla would eat and she was so quiet, like a blanket on the chair.

Carla was a picture of broken records scattered and spread out on the shore of the Pacific Ocean. She was as far away from living as she had ever been; she felt like she had already lived her entire life: leaving Alaska, the skyscraper, the plague, then losing Dodge. It all seemed to have taken fifty years from her.

In another room, leaning over the stove,

Joan watched the bubbles form in the white inside the pan, boil and steam. She pulled it off the burner and poured the hot milk into a cup.

Joan went quietly into the other room, up to Carla and she put the cup on the windowsill. "I made you something to drink," she broke the silence.

Carla was still in a crystal ball somewhere, but the hand on her shoulder brought her back, startled her to become aware of the rain on the windows again and the cup steaming in front of her.

It all wasn't just a dream, the last two days were past and she had to move on now. Still she remembered, "I dreamed about Dodge." She held the cup on her lap. "He didn't have to open the suit. He found a helicopter and attached the propellers to himself so he could fly. He flew along as we rode in the airship." She stared at Joan openly, "He probably could have done that too, he could build things like that." The vision disappeared like a torn apart cloud.

"I shouldn't have made him leave that suit," Carla said.

"No, Carla!" Joan pressed her hands into Carla's. "No, it's not your fault! You didn't do anything wrong. He had to leave it sometime, he couldn't hide forever."

"He was right though. He wasn't ready for the world. We should have waited," Carla was almost in tears again. "And I only saw him for a second."

"Oh Carla," Joan sighed.

"Now there's just sand inside of me too."

"I know," Joan said.

"I'm ready to leave." Carla held the hot cup on her knees and said, "Can we leave now?"

"We should wait until the rain ends. We can't see through these clouds."

"That's okay, it's only rain. I just want to leave." Carla looked out the birdcage windows. She waited for him to leave her eyes. "Do you know how a place can become full of a person you knew? The more I'm around here, the more I expect to see him. I even thought I saw his ghost out on the reservoir. We have to get away from here," Carla said, "because it's just too full of him."

"Okay." Joan moved from her side. "I'll get the airship ready for takeoff."

"Wait! I'll go with you. Don't leave me alone. Just help me get some things." She looked around herself, "Let me get my records, then we can go."

With a balancing act of stacks of records in their arms, they went through the garage to where the bicyclebird spread its wings next to a rotting Rolls Royce.

Carla said, "I need to bring this too. He made it for me."

Joan stared at the flightless bicycle in strange disbelief, "Yeah, I guess we could tie a line to it and pull it up." She lifted the handlebars, "It's big, but it's pretty light." She laughed, "Dodge made this?"

Carla nodded and put the records over the front tire, in the basket designed for them. She steered to the doorway and the wings rose ever slowly. The pedals turned against her. "It's still pouring."

They each held a handlebar grip and walked the bicyclebird out into the falling rain. When it rains in Seattle, it's a reminder that the world is 2/3 water; oceans and rivers of puddles and streams in the green.

Turning waterwheels flapped the wings up and down between them. It was a wet walk to the waiting airship.

When they stopped, Joan put her hand on the rope ladder, "I'll go up and lower you a line from the winch. You can tie the ends of the rope to the bicycle frame and climb up. Then we can pull it up."

She climbed hand over hand, going up quickly as a pirate in the rigging, but Carla kept her eyes on the ground.

That was the place Dodge stood before he disappeared.

She remembered dragging his empty metal shell away. It had taken them all of that watery day pulling the car parts to where Carla wanted to bury his remains in the reservoir. Ducks and pelicans floated over his rust and sand.

There was nothing left of him for her to hold but the bicyclebird.

The smallest figure of Joan crawled into the door of the ship and waved and the rope came down. Carla tied the lines to the machine.

Carla wasn't afraid of heights, she liked them, but she was no trapeze artist—climbing a rope ladder in the swinging wind and rain was no easy thing.

She stopped once, to say goodbye to all the ground she had known. Her arms were wrapped tightly in the ropes for safety. Carla could see patches in the clouds and fog.

The green land was drinking and feeding more roots and vines to grow further. The last frontier was turning into what it was in the beginning. The car lots were disappearing, blackberries were spreading out fast.

She climbed the rest of the way up and Joan helped her inside.

"Welcome aboard!" Joan smiled. She was wearing the obsolete uniform of an aircleaner pilot. It made her strange as a troubadour. "We'll bring that bicycle up then we can set sail." She switched controls starting the engines, one after the other in order across the dashboard.

Instrument panels, lights and controls and maps covered the walls around the windows. The floor was made of some kind of carpet their shoes seemed to cling to. Joan pressed the winch button near the doorway. It strained as it pulled on the rope.

Like a big anchor, Dodge's bicyclebird was drawn up next to the door, dripping rain off its white wings. They each took hold of it and had to turn it and twist it to pull it inside. The ship steadied once they were done and had locked the wheels to the floor.

"Now to get underway." Joan went to stand at the controls. Her hands were busy with buttons and levers. "It's going to be tricky. We have to release the holding wires and steer against this crosswind, so we aren't blown back into the towers."

The airship pitched to the left from the shock of docking wires letting go. Joan compensated, turning the wheel and running the engines full throttle.

Carla was pinned as the ship arose out of the radio towers until they leveled out. "Piece of cake!" she heard Joan say, but Carla was flattened to the floor.

Her nerves were fried, but she could move again. Getting up and holding her lost stomach, Carla arrived next to Joan.

Out the window, arctic gray clouds piled around them.

"Try looking through that screen there." Joan pointed at a black lens in the dashboard. A green sort of television light came from it.

Carla looked into it and saw shapes moving directly below. "I can see the ground!" she said, "Perfectly! I see the birds and all the trees!"

"Yeah, we used to need that when there was smog and we couldn't see. But it helps you see right through any kind of clouds."

"I can see the mansions and the park, all the birds on the reservoir."

Joan told her, "You can twist that dial to magnify things."

"The rain is still falling. I'm looking at the reservoir." Carla turned the dial and there in the shallows was the car shape of Dodge. But it isn't really him, she told herself; the sunken orange suit was a photograph, a battleship memory, a coral Pearl Harbor tragedy. She only ever saw the real him for a second.

Their reflection moved on chopping water.

Carla asked, "Are we over the ocean?"

"No, that's Lake Washington."

When Carla turned the knob, the magnified sight fell away and ocean took the shape of a lake. "Oh yes, I see. I was looking through it much too close! A car looks like a battleship."

"And a fish looks like a submarine." Joan laughed, "I know, you can thread a needle with that machine. It's best just to keep it set on the altitude we're at, which is about..." she leaned over and read a flashing dial. "Fifty feet!"

Furiously, Joan raked her hand over the console controls. The engines roared. "Hold on!"

A crash shook them as they hit water, bouncing off the surface of the lake, back into the air. "Yikes!" She pulled the wheel and drove them out of the dive. "We're lucky the ship stayed together!" she yelled over the engine howl. "Carla, if you didn't notice our altitude, we'd be smashed into pieces all over the lake."

"Are you sure you know how to fly this thing?" Carla was gripping the seat cushion as if they had crashed already and she clung to it like a life preserver…with sharks circling her. "I hope you do!"

"It's okay. This is just different than driving in the city, on some preset pollution pattern. That's what I'm used to. That's like driving a subway train compared to this. Everything's under control now. Look, we're at two hundred feet."

"What about skyscrapers?" Carla knew the lake would be ending soon and the land beginning, with all its tall monuments. They had gone from disaster to disaster, from the Titanic to The Towering Inferno.

"Don't worry, Carla. We're gaining more altitude just in case."

Carla hoped the reason Joan's flying was such a rodeo was just because of the cowboy boots she wore.

The floor got steep again and Carla slid. Her ears were snapping. She tried to calm herself, to assess the situation as calmly as Dodge would have. "Are we safe now?" She swallowed and tried to clear the pressure in her ears.

Joan began to smooth out their climb. She said, "Try out that magnifier again," pointing her decorated sleeve, "See what you can see."

Carla could walk once more, back to the magnifying screen. Noticing how much she was shaking, she begged Joan, "Let's just be more careful please. I've already had a lifetime of excitement."

"We won't have any more obstacles." Joan held the wheel level, "We'll just circle at a safe height."

Carla studied the magnifying screen. It was filled with movement. Before she said anything though, she adjusted the lens to make sure she wasn't seeing an anthill at close range. "There's something happening down there," she said. "But I can't figure out what it is."

Joan kept a hand to steady the wheel and leaned over to look at the screen. "We're over the farm factories. But that doesn't seem right—it looks like they're still operating."

The miles of blurring machinery down below were moving and steam and hot flames poured out of their smokestacks.

"It's all still running and it's still polluting!

The machines haven't stopped!" Carla cried, "Is that what got Dodge?"

"No, I don't think so. I'm not getting anything out of the ordinary." Joan turned the wheel and started a slow descent; the walls rattled as she steered. "We'll see what's going on. I'll connect to their landing beacon."

The sound of pinging sonar filled the room, getting louder.

"There, we're locked on."

Carla stared at the wavelength lights. "There must be a reason the factories are still running." If only Sherlock Holmes could appear in this mixed up tragedy...

Joan said, "There must be people who need things."

The heartbeating sonar got faster as they got closer and continued to fall. Gray clouds broke on the windows. Flying through the cover they could see momentarily down to the valley. Rain streaked across the windows.

"I remember this place," Joan said. "I had to do sweeping over it when I first started out." She added, "Still looks the same though."

The ship was under the control of the landing beacon, which slowed their descent and guided them into a docking gate. Robot docking arms reached out from the terminal building and took hold of the aircleaner. The engines shut off automatically. The cabin was quiet.

Joan switched off some buttons. That was it. "Let's go take a look at Mechafarms Incorporated. I'm sure they'll be surprised to see us."

The elevated walkway hit against the hull and the ship rocked.

Carla whispered. "We don't know who's out there. We don't know what they want."

Joan shrugged, about to say something, when the door opened by itself, steam hissing around the edges. She was glad Carla was next to her.

The empty hallway tunnel to the terminal blinked with white flickering lights. So far there was no greeting party.

Joan went into the hall with Carla following.

Out the portholes, a city of machinery chugged like steamboats in the rain.

"This is the way to the control room." Joan put her hand on the doorknob and turned it. The door swung open to reveal computers and chattering read-out machines, all working by themselves.

"There's no one here." Carla walked around the seats. No sign of the workers. The read-outs were hieroglyphics to her: dots, dashes and crooked figures.

Joan was reading a machine, "Carla! This whole place is automated! It's been running itself the whole time. Look!" She pressed a button and flicked through different views of factory operations. Everything had its own life.

Tended by robots, assembly lines poured red iron from the furnaces, cooled it and turned it into shapes to stack at the other end. Wheels and gears turned and turned.

But everything stopped when Joan pulled the master switch.

O

The sky was crystal clear and blue. They sailed in an airstream far above the ground.

Carla felt like a migrating bird. She didn't need the viewscreen anymore; she leaned out of a window with a telescope. "Let's fly across America forever."

An interstate highway ran underground into a field, a few car wrecks were tossed on its edges. The entire countryside seemed to be returning to prairie. A herd of buffalo left a cloud as they ran.

"I don't see anything but land and animals and ruins," Carla called.

Joan was watching the sky from the observation deck outside. "Well, come out here and see this. There's smoke on the horizon."

"Not another factory?" Carla walked out into the breeze.

"No, I don't think so."

Carla pointed the telescope at the threads of smoke. From the plain on the horizon, the smoke drifted up and curled. She gave Joan a chance to see.

In the valley below, cooking fires from tents and teepees sent up a quiet smoke.

"Look at all the tents!" Carla laughed, "Are that many people down there? We just had to get away from the city to find them! They're gathering all around below us!"

The crowd took up the fallen landing lines and pulled the airship. Wooden stakes hammered the lines into the earth. Pulling the ropes in hand over hand, they dragged the airship down.

It was too bad Joan chose this place to land.

But how would she have known?

Joan flung the door open, "Fellow Americans!" she greeted them.

How could she have known what was waiting?

They grabbed her and pulled her outside.

Carla was next. They held her arms behind her back as she struggled.

"We regret to inform you..." a man told Joan, "We must destroy your ship."

"What?" Joan shook off the arms holding her. "We need our ship! You can't do that! Look, if we made a mistake showing up here, we're sorry. It won't happen again. I'll move it, we'll leave. We'll fly away and never come back."

"Give me a torch," the man demanded.

"I've seen you before," Carla told him. "I used to see your picture all over the city. You're Gary Justice!"

"No I'm not," he said quickly. He motioned to the people behind him, "Burn the ship!"

"Wait!"

Gary Justice gave them a choice, "You'll either have to join us, or leave here on foot. Your airship isn't allowed. We're erasing every trace of old America."

"Why?" Joan struggled.

He explained in that familiar TV voice, "Everything old must go. We have to make room for the new America."

More people with fire were circling the ship.

Joan got an arm free and pushed them away from her. She fought to get to the airship's doorway.

Seeing her chance, Carla ducked through their arms and slipped back inside. Ragged people were already smashing the controls with wooden hammers.

She grabbed the bicyclebird and pushed it out the doors on the other side. A long field rolled ahead of her. Jumping onto the seat, she started to pedal and move faster, hoping Dodge didn't really forget about gravity—not in this time of need.

She didn't get far.

It would have been an amazing escape if hands didn't grab her from behind and pull on the bicycle wheels, stopping the wings from churning.

Through the confusion, Joan was dragged up next to her and held tight.

Gary Justice didn't delay. He took a step forward and threw the torch into the open door. It caught on the spilled maps and clothes. Flames went across the floor, up the walls.

"No!" Joan tried wrestling with them, but it was no use. She was forced to watch the fire spread. Out the doors and across the trestling of the observation deck, the fire reached up the airframe and caught on the fabric skin.

The heat roared. Black smoke sent the crowd back, and Joan and Carla were let free.

Witnessing her airship's Hindenburg funeral, the white heat of the collapsed and melted shape, the charred remains left cooling like a beached whale skeleton washed up in the field, Joan told Carla, "At least I didn't go down with the ship."

Only one person was able to move from that candle. Gary Justice wasn't done yet. He pointed at the bicyclebird, "Now that other machine must be burned."

"Just a minute!" Joan gave Carla a push and hissed, "Go!"

Carla hopped on. She heard Joan explain, "It wasn't built during America. It was built afterwards. It's a new thing!" This time, with Joan protecting her, the bicyclebird began to move.

The wings bellowed up and down.

Pedaling faster and faster, the crowds fell away but she could hear them yelling. Their voices seemed to disappear off a cliff.

The wings were hopping the bike in and out of the air and Carla was straining to keep it going over the bumpy field. She was far away from them now, but she wanted to try to get the machine into the air completely and stay that way.

The tall grass shocked over in her wake as she bounced, flying and landing, flying again. She could smell the salt breeze of the ocean; she could hear the surf crashing a long way below, flying with seagulls as the land wasn't beneath her anymore.

O

(part two)

THE SAND RIVERS

She saw herself, brought back in time and trying vainly to convince people where the future was taking them. Why would anyone believe her? Maybe she would end up watching history repeat itself, like a film she'd seen before. But she had to try.

For this reason, she opened the time machine door, just for a moment, but it was too late, she had already slipped through time, back to America.

O

The time machine was a metal box like a large safe, with a door that unlatched on the side. There was nothing inside but a ledge to sit on. The floor, ceiling and walls were all the same gray stainless steel. She had no idea how it operated, she just sat down and closed the door gently.

O

The wings carried Carla to shore. She was washed up in a tidal pool. Two pale feathered hands held her lying in the middle. Waves went over her and spread her fingers in the sea anemones. Fish darted in and out of the folds in her clothes.

The rest of the broken bicyclebird was crumpled metal under thirty feet of water, off shore.

A blue bruise colored her temple. Her black hair washed around like seaweed. Carla had been unconscious, moved safely from the waves onto the sand without even knowing.

Finally, her eyes broke the Ophelia spell and opened.

She saw the beach slanting away under the cliffs and clouds.

Carla remembered. She remembered the flight, when the bicycle wheels went off the cliff edge and the wings took over, moving her in the sky. Half bicycle and half bird, Dodge had made an amazing flying machine for her. Even though he warned her, "I forgot about gravity," back when she laughed and rode it on lawns instead of over ocean, the bicyclebird worked.

Carla turned her head on the sand and groaned. Slowly, her hand crawled to the bump on her forehead.

The crash.

When she was too tired to keep the wings flapping, down she went. *She* was the one who forgot about gravity.

She tried to sit up, but fell back onto the feathers. There was a light show in front of her eyes. The pain went away if she was still. So she rested…while the tide went out and left her to dry, shipwrecked with disintegrating wings.

When the sun was setting into the Pacific, she woke up cold and rolled off the wings, onto the beach. "Here I am, starting over again," she thought. Starting again with even less than before. Now all she had was some white feathers and what she wore.

She stood up slowly. The world rocked and weaved. Leaning back down, she picked up the light wings and shook out the sand.

Records were scattered on the beach; music was coming ashore like scallops. She picked up a half moon of vinyl and sighed. Broken. It was a good one.

The stars were blinking on overhead, as the sky got dark and a small light on the rocks far down the beach opened and shut its bright eye.

There was no reason for a lighthouse to be operating in this new America, there were no ships on the water; there only seemed to be a few survivors and they were busy dismantling America. But it sure looked like a lighthouse; a revolving light in a tower.

So with the wings draped over her shoulders, Carla walked towards what she hoped was a lighthouse with hot food piled on a galley table. She was dizzy from hunger. The last time she ate was with Joan...Joan…Where had she gone? That seemed longer than a long time ago when they were together, a thousand feet above sea level, a shadow on the clouds.

Along the shoreline, tangles of blackberries grew. She picked handfuls as she walked until the sand finally ended in rocky breakwater.

Caught in the candlepower at the foot of the lighthouse, she stood there wearing wings, with blood red juice on her hands and the wind turning the sea into storm.

O

He thought he was looking at an angel. She

was about to fall and he ran out and caught her before she landed on the rocks.

O

"It's not easy to fool a magician," he said as she woke up. "I thought you were an angel."

Trick flowers sprung up around her, all around the curved walls of the lighthouse room. Bright sunlight filled the space. She could hear the ocean. There were photographs, posters and diplomas on the walls. She reached from the covers and felt the bandage on her head. Her eyes closed again.

O

When she reawakened, there was a record player on the table next to her. The walls had changed too—he had redecorated with her washed ashore wings and records, held up with strings and nails.

She sat up in bed.

Carryin' On with Johnny Cash and June Carter sat on the turntable. She picked up the arm and set the needle on the vinyl. A sandy scratch, then music filled the round room.

The next song was beginning when there was a knocking on the door.

"Come in," she said. She remembered his voice.

He was wearing a black suit with tails and a top-hat. She remembered him saying something about a magician. Smiling, he took the hat off and pulled out a rabbit. It sat in the crook of his arm while he pet it. "I'm glad you're finally awake, Carla."

"Thanks for helping me," she smiled back. Then, "How did you know my name?"

"You were talking in your sleep. That's how I knew about your records too. I spent all day out on the sand and in the breakers, saving all I could." He pointed at the record player and laughed, "I had that down in the basement."

"Thank you. This is your lighthouse? Is there anyone else here?"

"Just you and me and my assistant." He put the rabbit back in the black hat and replaced it on his head. "It's been so long I saw anyone. I even tried magic to make someone appear from thin air."

"Well, it worked," she laughed. "Here I am, just like magic! So, what's your name?"

She expected him to say, The Great-someone-or-other.

"It doesn't matter what you call me now, names don't mean anything anymore. Things have changed."

"Oh, come on!" Carla poked him, "Don't be so mysterious, Mister Magician. What did you used to be called?"

"I would rather not be called anything."

"But what used to be your name?"

He reached in his pocket and took out a fan of cards. He looked them over carefully. "That was a long time ago, that's not me anymore. Now that you're here, I want to be someone else. I've changed."

"We've all changed," Carla said.

"I haven't decided on a new name."

"Alright," she paused, "how about The Incredible Lifesaving Lighthouse Keeper Magician?"

"That's fine...Maybe something a little shorter, but I like that."

She laughed.

He took a silver coin from behind her ear and he held it up before her eyes.

"In Carla We Trust," she read the shiny inscription aloud. She took the coin from his hand, "Thanks, Magician."

"You're welcome, Carla. Thanks for showing up here."

She decided she would stay. "I showed up because I saw your light," Carla said.

He said, "The last lighthouse in America, I guess. Seven floors including the basement—here, let me show you around. I know you're not afraid of heights." He led her into the spiral stairwell and they went up.

She kept close to him. She would touch his arm or shoulder.

They met in the light of the reflected lens at the top.

O

When morning found them, finally arriving with a red sky over the hills, he was so tired. He couldn't show her anymore of his world. He said, "We should maybe think about getting some sleep." There was no more of the lighthouse that she hadn't seen. The white rabbit from his hat curled sleeping at the end of their bed.

O

"Never play pinball with a magician, Carla."
The steel ball went wherever he commanded it.
It followed his finger, it lit up every light on the
machine.

"You're cheating!" she pushed him.

"No I'm not! It's magic." He laughed. He
was racking up millions of points.

"It's not fair!"

"Fair?" With his fingertip pressed to the
glass, he held the ball magnetized. When the
ball rolled again, it hit the flipper and he shot
for 100,000 points.

"I don't know why you spend your time on
pinball."

"I needed something to keep me company
before you appeared."

Carla turned away from him and his game.
There was no point playing with him. Leaving
the magician to himself, she went to the other
pinball machine.

With its chrome and reflectors and glass like
a windshield, it looked like a car.

"Hey! Where did this come from?" she
called.

"I found both of them in town. I don't

think that one works. You want to come back and play a game with me?" Then he checked himself, tipping his top-hat, "No, of course you don't." He smiled.

When she touched the pinball game, it re-acted with car horns and flashing headlights. It wanted her attention.

It was no surprise.

She already knew why. "Dodge?" she whispered.

Words flashed across the top of the game where the Hi-Scores were listed. CARLA, CARLA, CARLA...Like a tickertape, her name flashed.

"No, this can't be. This isn't happening..." Her words drifted off into the traffic jam sound of the machine. "You're not Dodge, you're not! You can't be."

IT'S ME!

DODGE!

CARLA, IS THAT REALLY YOU?

CARLA?

She took a step backwards.

I DON'T KNOW HOW IT HAPPENED

SOMEHOW I'M A PINBALL MACHINE

The words blinked on the panel. Every sentence repeated so she could see it again and it made her cry even more. She turned to the magician, "What is this machine?" Sobbing, "What is this game?" Did the magician know? Was she talking in her sleep about Seattle?

He left his pinball game and stood beside her. "I don't know." He stroked the tears away from her cheeks. "What's the matter?"

She couldn't stop crying, "It's been spelling out words! It's talking to me like someone I know."

The display panel was flashing scores again.

"The later models were given talking function to make is seem more like a real opponent." He brushed the hair around her ear. "They're just programmed words."

"No, it wrote my name. It knew my name and...How could it know those things?"

"What's the matter, Carla? Why are you so sad?" Daubing her tears with an endless rainbow colored handkerchief dragged from his jacket pocket, he told her, "It's just a machine, dear. There's probably something wrong with its program. Just random letters..."

"No! It knows me."

"Forget about it, Carla. Come on, let's play the other game again. I'll play with a handicap. I'll stand on one leg."

"No," she pointed to the stars shooting across the display. "We know each other."

"A pinball machine?"

"He used to be a car," she dried her eyes with the back of her hand. "He was a person in a car suit. I told you about him."

"Dodge..." the magician said dryly, "I wish you wouldn't talk about him. I thought he turned to dust."

"I still remember him," she put her hand on the game, "He meant a lot to me."

The magician hovered over the car-shaped pinball game. "I don't know, Carla," but when he pressed the flipper levers, the machine suddenly lost power. "He must have blown a fuse. If it *is* Dodge, that is. If it is him, he's better than The Great Houdini."

"It is him." She leaned her head onto the machine and listened carefully. "He told me he somehow became a pinball machine."

The magician paused, "It would be quite the performance to transfer yourself into something new."

Carla tried to find something of him in the metal and glass. "When he made that carsuit," she remembered, "maybe he designed something into it that would allow him to escape again. I only saw him for a flash second then he disappeared."

The magician was examining the machine for secret buttons, or hidden parts. "There's got to be some way he did it," he mumbled, searching the chrome.

"Look, he's talking again!" she pointed at the screen.

IT REALLY IS ME
DODGE
I STILL HAVE NOT FIGURED OUT WHY
BUT I HAVE BEEN GIVEN LIFE AGAIN
AS A PINBALL MACHINE
"Dodge? Can you hear me?"
YES CARLA
I CAN SEE YOU TOO
YOU ARE WEARING A GREEN SWEATER

"Dodge?" She tugged her knitted sweater sleeve. "You're more of a machine than ever now. How will I ever get you out of this?"

REINCARNATED AS A PINBALL MA-CHINE
"You didn't plan this?"
NO
HOW COULD I POSSIBLY PLAN

THIS?

"That's true," Carla agreed and laughed, sniffed.

"But maybe you inadvertently designed an escape mechanism into your suit." The magician was wondering ways of doing that. "It would take a real wizard to send yourself into a machine...Although I can't expect you to tell us how you did it." He smiled, "It's our well known code that a magician will never reveal his illusion."

NO, THIS WAS JUST LUCK

O

Moonlight. Carla crept out of the bedroom and down the circling stairway. It curled to the ground floor.

The lights were blinking on the pinball machines. They always were. She could see her way over to the car-shaped one.

"Dodge?" she whispered.

When she got close to him, he told her a story, just like he used to. When she couldn't sleep, she would go to the garden and he would make something up for her, or tell her a sleepy fairy tale.

She put her hands on him and read his words.

WHEN SHE WAS CAST UNDER A SPELL

THE WALLS AROUND HER BECAME A CASTLE

AND SHE WAS KEPT PRISONER

UNDER MOSS AND COLD MIST

ONLY HER DREAMS LEFT OUT THE WINDOW

FLOATED FROM THE CASTLE LIKE BIRDS AT NIGHT

AND QUIETLY TRAVELED OVER HILLS AND RIVERS

UNTIL ONE EARLY MORNING BEFORE SUNRISE

HER DREAMS CAUGHT A STRONG BREEZE

TRAVELED VERY FAR TO AN OCEAN

LANDED ON A ROOF AND WENT INTO A ROOM

WHERE SHE FOUND HIM SLEEPING

AND SUDDENLY HE SAW HER

SHE WAS SO CLEAR TO HIM

IN THE MORNING WHEN HE WOKE

HE TOOK A BUS TO THE CAR RENTAL AGENCY

GOT IN A BRAND NEW CADILLAC
WITH WHITE WALLS
    AND DROVE FOR DAYS AND NIGHTS
TO FIND HER

Then the lights fell to a warm glow.

"Dodge..." Carla softly whispered. She lay her head on the glass of him. She looked back up to his screen and wiped her eyes.

Dodge quickly turned back into numbers and scores.

"Dodge?" she asked. "Are you still there?"

It was the magician who spoke from behind her, "What are you doing down here, Carla? Playing pinball?"

"Yes!"

"You're crying," he came over to her. "What's the matter?" he said, putting his hands over her shoulders.

"Nothing," she said. "I just lost a game."

"You should leave this pinball machine alone." He pulled her away and back to him. "There's something wrong with it."

She turned from him to read the numbers flashing on the screen.

"There's something I have to tell you, Carla. This is important, dear."

"What?"

"This is just a machine...It's not Dodge. I have to be honest," he lied. "I programmed it to seem like him. I put in everything you told me about him."

She stared hard into the magician's eyes. "What?"

"I thought it would cheer you up. So I re-programmed the machine... It's only numbers and letters, that's all. I did it myself. There is no Dodge anymore." He tried to kiss her, but her face moved away.

She shook off his hands and pulled away. "That can't be."

"Yes, Carla. I'm sorry, I shouldn't have done it. I didn't think it would affect you like this. I'm sorry, Carla. I didn't know how you felt. Come on, Carla," he held out his arms to her. "Come on, let's go back upstairs."

She stood there with the red lights playing on her.

The magician waited for her. He sighed. "Come on, Carla. It's just a machine, honestly. Come with me..." He reached over to her and took her hand, "Carla...Lets go."

She felt like she was being dragged away, but only part of her was going with him.

O

While the magician was a tiny figure fishing on the shore, she went back inside the lighthouse and hurried to the pinball machine. "Dodge?" she said. "It's me, Carla. He's gone, we can talk."

HI CARLA

"Oh, Dodge! I wish you were here."

I AM WITH YOU

THIS IS AS CLOSE AS I CAN BE RIGHT NOW

"Can't you find a way to get to me? I need to be with you."

I'LL FIND A WAY, CARLA

YOU KNOW THAT I WILL

Maybe he would, or maybe he would just travel from machine to machine.

O

That night the waves crashed over the rocks below. Storms approached. It took a long time before the magician was asleep. Carla lay there awake, listening to his breathing. Finally, she slipped out from under blankets, moving quiet

190

as she could to the stairwell.

A minute later she touched the pinball machine and woke up Dodge.

His lights blinked with, CARLA! HOW ARE YOU?

"Not so good, Dodge. I need you to come to my rescue. You have to find a way out of this."

I'M TRYING, I'M TRYING

I JUST DON'T WANT TO FAIL

I COULD END UP INSIDE THE TOASTER

OR WORSE

Carla rested her cheek on him, "Please, Dodge. All I can think about is you." She stared into the lights in him, "You're real aren't you? I have to know that you're real."

OF COURSE I'M REAL

FEAR NOT, CARLA

I'LL FIND A WAY TO YOU

"How?" She was starting to cry again, "I can't take much more of this, Dodge."

I KNOW. IT'S DIFFICULT FOR ME TOO, CARLA

IT'S NOT EASY BEING IN THE WRONG BODY

ESPECIALLY WHEN YOU ARE A

PINBALL MACHINE
ALL I WANT IS TO BE WITH YOU, CARLA

"All I want is to be with you, Dodge. Why does it have to be so hard?"

DON'T WORRY, WE'RE NEARLY THERE

"I miss you, Dodge! I don't know what I'm supposed to do without you. I feel like I'm dying. I wish and I wish and I wish."

"Carla?" the magician was calling for her from the stairs, coming down.

"Oh, no," she whispered, "I have to hide, Dodge! I love you!" She ran into the shadows, slid down behind a chair.

"Carla? Are you down here?"

The lantern showed the magician moving in the room, his silhouette dragged along the walls.

She clutched to the shadows.

"Carla?" He couldn't see her, but she could hear his footsteps taking him over to the Dodge pinball machine. "You've caused enough trouble," he told the game. "What are you trying to do? Steal Carla away from me? How? You're a pinball machine!" He laughed. "But just to make sure, I'm getting you out of here."

Carla caught herself from springing up.

The magician rattled keys, "You can stay locked in the basement. You can rot down there and turn into rust."

Carla brushed the shadows aside as he grabbed the pinball machine and started to drag it.

"No!" Carla jumped out into the light of the lantern. "Don't take him away!" She grabbed the magician's arm.

The lantern threw their crazy shadows along the wall, two people fighting over pinball.

Carla fell back against the wall and cried, "Dodge! Do something!"

"Forget about him!" the magician told her. He got on the other side of the game and pushed it towards the door. "He's gone forever."

Another step towards the basement door and everything blinked.

Blue lightning crackled out of Dodge, tracing its bite all around the magician.

Carla saw the magician fall to the floor.

O

WHAT ELSE WAS I SUPPOSED TO DO?

"He helped me. He was here for me when I needed someone." She stared at the lifeless body of the magician, "I did love him too...It's alright to tell you that, isn't it?"

Dodge was gone. The screen had turned back into the numbers.

"Dodge?" she asked, frightened. "Dodge, are you there?"

From behind her, the magician stirred. Slowly realigning himself with reality, he coughed and called, "Carla?" He could see her nearby. "Help me, Carla...I'm hurt..."

She got to her feet. I'm not moving, she thought. It's not me. He's hypnotizing me. Don't go to him, Carla, she told herself. But she was walking to his side and she spoke without meaning to, "I'm sorry. Are you alright?"

He embraced her to him.

"I'm so sorry that happened." She told him other words that weren't hers. They weren't the words she felt. She couldn't explain how she felt. Her mind was flying itself away; she wasn't a part of this happening.

"I know, Carla. I'm horribly jealous. Now that I found you, I don't want to lose you." He took another breath, "I need rest. Help me upstairs, Carla." His weight was on her; using her legs to get him up the spiral to the bedroom.

She led him to bed and pulled the covers over him and she lay next to him to help him sleep.

I'm not here, she was thinking over and over. This isn't happening to me. I'm not here anymore.

O

In the early morning, the magician dressed in his black suit. She pretended to be asleep, not watching him as he walked to the stairs and went down.

Carla hopped out of the bed and hurried to the railing. The black shape of him was disappearing to the first floor. She knew where he was going, to get rid of Dodge. And she knew that heavy sound of the basement door. "No!" she screamed as she ran downstairs.

The magician was pushing the pinball machine over the floor, the last few feet to the dark doorway falling into the basement.

She screamed again.

The machine toppled into blackness, a terrible crashing, on its steep landslide way to the stone basement floor.

Carla ran after Dodge and the magician knew his fears were true.

He wasn't the one.

He slammed the door on them and turned the key.

He heard her scream, but he left the room. He carried the key outside, past the breakwater and across the low tide sand. The eel grass was laid flat. He went to the line of surf and threw the key as far as he could.

O

Carla couldn't beat against the door anymore. At the bottom of the stairs, the Dodge pinball game was twisted and broken. She moved carefully in the blackness until she could feel him again.

"Dodge...Are you still there? You can't be gone..." Her hands went slowly over the broken metal and jumped from the sharp glass. "Dodge? You can't just leave me here. You're still there, I know it. Please! Do something to help me. I don't want to die here! Dodge!"

There was a flicker of weak red light on

the screen above her face. The scores flickered in a candle-like way and then she could read Dodge's thoughts.

CARLA

"Dodge!" She got up off the cold floor and leaned over him, to be closer to his words. "Dodge, are you alright?!"

I FEEL LIKE I DON'T HAVE TOO MUCH LONGER

"Dodge, don't disappear. I need you!" She tried to put her strength into him, if only she could. "Dodge, why did you leave me and let him come back?"

I THOUGHT THAT WAS WHAT YOU WANTED

"No! That's not what I wanted...I didn't *know* what I wanted, then..." She looked around the red gloom of the moss and stones and cold dripping walls. "How are we going to get out of here?"

CARLA

I CAN SAVE YOU

BUT IT MAY BE THE END OF ME

She had to read it again.

CARLA

STAND BEHIND ME

His words were fading out.

"What are you going to do?" Her feet crunched on debris. "We both have to get out of this together."

I'M A MACHINE

AND I'M RUNNING DOWN

I'VE BEEN BROKEN BEYOND REPAIR

SO LET ME DO THIS LAST THING FOR YOU

CARLA

THIS IS THE WAY OUT

PLEASE STAND BACK

She stepped around him, "I'll find a way to help you too, Dodge. Somehow—"

A blue shock of lightning streaked out of him, up the stairs and hit the oak door, splintering it and blowing a big hole.

He didn't have to tell her to hurry.

She ran up the stones and ducked through the smoking door remains. Across the bright room, the front door was open, the sea air blew inside and she ran.

Her feet landed on the sand outside. The way was clear to the blackberry bushes and trees.

O

The problem was, she didn't know where to go next. Hiding in the blackberry clearing, she could see the tall lighthouse in the distance.

She lay back flat and looked up through the vines and berries. Bees overhead, a spider hanging in the center of its web, she felt safe inside this space.

Seagulls and the rolling sound of the waves coming ashore.

"Carla..." her name floated up from the beach. The magician was calling her, "Carla!"

She sat up and peered through the sharp green.

The dot of him moved along the sand, following the footsteps she had made when she escaped.

"Oh no!"

"Carla!" He was getting closer. "Carla, I'm sorry...Wherever you are, I'm sorry! Come back." The magician held a bouquet of white flowers, popped from his black hat. "Carla, I made a mistake! I wasn't going to leave you down there. I lost my temper."

He stopped at the thick edge of the black-berries, where her footsteps ended like a rabbit running in to hide.

"Carla! Please forgive me. I'm sorry! I won't ever hurt you again. Please come back!" He waited there, looking into the vines and listening.

She was sure that he could see her, she closed her eyes and tucked herself down close to the sand. If only she could disappear.

"Carla, if you're in there...I want you to know I'm so deeply sorry. You can come back to the lighthouse. The door will be open...You don't want to spend the night in the cold. It's going to rain tonight. I'll make dinner for you... It will be waiting for you. I'll keep it warm... Please Carla..."

The magician kneeled and put flowers on the sand in front of the blackberries. "I never meant to hurt you. I love you, Carla." He stood back up, "I'll be waiting for you, Carla." Then he said in a mumble, "I know you, Carla. I know you'll be back."

She stared at the sand between her hands. She was so hurt and confused and tired. The soft grains leaked through her fingers and became the ground again.

He walked back to the lighthouse, slowly, in his top hat and black suit.

Carla sat up to make sure he was going back. It was getting dark. She saw the door stay open. The amber light at the top was circling for the ships lost at sea.

That was her last view of the lighthouse.

She crawled from her hiding space, hand over hand, out of the thick patch of berries and she stood up on the other side. It made a sharp wall between her and him.

Another new world was beginning. She just started walking, into the woods. Wherever it would take her was good.

O

She followed the road in the moonlight. The forest on either side was scary, but it was taking her somewhere. That was all she cared about. Black trees looked down at her as she walked on the crumbled tar.

O

For some time she could see the form of it sitting in the road ahead. A nighttime mirage,

201

a spell of owls, the full moon's pantomime.

Nearly there, she could tell what it was.

A car.

Good. That's helpful. She didn't care about driving it, she just wanted to sleep somewhere. She opened the back door of the station wagon and looked inside. It was empty, not even any sand remains. "Good," she said, crawling onto the vinyl seat and pulling the door closed.

O

Carla jumped awake. Nightmares in the back of a car.

Morning.

Sitting up, she rubbed her hands on her cheeks, her eyes, and yawned. The car was parked sideways, blocking the road. It pointed deep into the woods. On the dashboard were crushed cans of Double Diet Cola and some spilled beads. The keys were in the ignition.

She crawled over the back seat and sat behind the wheel.

The car started on the first try.

"Hurray!"

She turned the wheel and stepped on the

gas. The car jumped forward like an animal.

Because she always drove with music, Carla turned on the radio.

"Hello again, Carla!" the radio greeted her in a familiar voice.

The last time she heard that voice, it came from inside a different machine.

"Dodge?" She nearly went off the road. "Dodge!"

"Hi, Carla...I guess I'm a car radio now."

She laughed and turned him up.

"How did that happen?" she gleamed.

"I don't know...It's all very strange."

"Dodge!" She laughed. He was a radio beside the speedometer, "We made it!"

She gave the car more gas and it bumped faster.

He laughed back, "Care for a song, Carla? I take requests."

O

"Couldn't you have picked a better car to be reincarnated into, Dodge?" she asked. "Why not a sports car? Wouldn't you rather be flying along in something flashy? Instead, you end up in a junky station wagon with bad shock absorbers..." The road was an ancient bounce. "I'd call that bad karma!" she smiled.

"Thanks, Carla." He crackled with static, "I'm just glad to be alive again."

"By the way, how does it feel to be a radio?"

"Not too different from a pinball game, I guess. It's hard to describe what being alive is like. Especially life as a machine...You just are."

She steered past another gas station. "It's a good thing there are so many gas stations left over. As long as this car holds up, we can keep driving...wherever we're driving to."

"Where exactly *are* we going, Carla?" the radio asked her.

Ahead of them, the road was covered over by gray.

"Straight into that sand," she pointed down the hood.

O

"There shouldn't be a desert here," Dodge said.

The car was stopped on the sand. The driver's door was open and Carla stood outside and

204

listened. There was something more than the sound of the wind pushing over the sand.

The murmur wasn't just a noise, the sand was talking; crowds of voices were talking from the river of sand that moved across the land.

O

More days of dust across the road as she drove and the backseat of the car was filled with water in jars. She thought she was dreaming when that lake first appeared, but she found out when she stopped that the mirage was real. There was even a gas station in the sand on the shore. She left there confident she was prepared. She had all the water she needed to drink and if the car ran out of gas, it would become a new oasis cup. Eventually, plants and trees would grow through the metal.

The open window wasn't much relief, rippling over hot waves on her sleeve, gusting a black curve of tickling hair across her eyes. Not that there was much to see besides desert.

A goldfish bowl rocked on the dashboard. In it, a lake minnow levitated.

She leaned over and looked through its

water. From the fish's point of view, the dry road went on forever, submerged like a river.

If she wanted to, she could have tied the steering wheel in place and just kept some weight on the pedal. On and on.

She couldn't tell if they were driving in circles, or if the desert went all the way across what used to be America.

There was no sound from the radio, Dodge was asleep.

She tried to see further into the horizon, but it all looked exactly the same, just further away.

O

"A ghost town," Carla told Dodge. "Just in time, too. The gas is on reserve."

She steered along the bending telephone poles towards the dark blur formed on the desert. The colorful signs of gas stations began to take shape out of it. Tilting roofs draped with dead electrical wires, sand making a Venice out of all the streets.

Carla filled the gas tank and they toured the dead places, getting food and even finding some records in a Goodwill store.

The day slipped into night and she parked in a field of sand.

Carla lay across the roof, on a mattress covered with blankets, her head resting on a pillow.

"I wish I still had my record player," she said. The doors were open so Dodge could hear her. "I'd put it right there on the hood. Music would play over us."

Dodge said, "Remember back in Seattle when I put all those speakers in the trees?"

"Yes," she smiled, picturing the birdhouse look of them.

"I wanted to surprise you!"

"You did! My records carried all through that park." She looked around her, "This place could sure use some of that."

She was watching the sky before she fell asleep.

A light dragged in the sky among all the millions of stars.

"Make a wish, Dodge. There goes a shooting star."

It wasn't though. It was a rocket, the same one Dodge had been waiting for; the one returning from the moon.

She watched it curve on to the horizon, until it blinked out of sight.

O

The smell of the burning town woke her up.

"Dodge!" she jumped out of the blankets, and fell onto her feet on the ground. Black clouds surrounded the car. "Wake up! The town's on fire!"

Across the sand, the shouting of two men carrying torches, dropping fire against a grocery store. The flames rippled along.

"We have to get out of here, Dodge!" She hopped into the car and turned the ignition. "Remember those people who burned Joan's aircleaner? They're here!" The engine roared and the car spun across the dust.

"Gary Justice?" Dodge asked in stereo.

"Yeah, that's him. He's got a following and it looks like they found us again!"

More of them ran from the station wagon, spreading the fires.

"Well, let's get out of here!"

"I'm trying!" Carla told him.

The car skidded around a burning,

collapsed billboard, driving over smashed glass and plastic, jagged concrete. That's what did it—the tires tore and Carla could barely hold the shaking wheel. "Dodge!"

Waves of flames, smoke, everything shimmered in the heat.

"Carla, save yourself!"

"No, Dodge. I can't leave you again!"

"Don't worry about me, Carla!" There was static in his voice. "You know I'll be back again as something else. Go find somewhere to hide. Try a bank—that's sure to be fireproof. I might be the telephone ringing inside. I'll tell you I'm alright. Now hurry, go!"

"I love you, Dodge!" She threw the door open and ran into the oven of the burning ghost town.

Just like he said, she wasn't far from a bank. Orange petals of fire grew along the path.

The door handle burned her hand as she opened it.

She crawled across the floor below the smoke. The vault was in the back of the room. The heavy steel door was left open.

Holding her blistered hand, she squeezed into the dim light of the safe. The floor was covered with dollars and paper checks, scattered everywhere.

"Dodge. You're gone again." She could hear the town outside burning away.

A tired voice answered her from the darkness. "I don't think I'll ever be a person again, Carla."

"Dodge?" She didn't know if she was laughing or crying. "You're back again! What are you now?" She reached into the dark furthest part of the vault. "Are you a talking cash register? A robot bank teller?"

Her hands held out for him, touched metal. "Are you part of the safe?" She felt around his solid box shape. "Dodge? What are you?"

"I'm getting tired of being machines," said the ex-pinball game, one-time car radio, lost human Dodge. "Now at least I'm finally a machine that can really help you."

"Dodge, what are you?" Her hands ran over him and around him.

"I'm a time machine."

She found a door on him. Her breathing echoed. In the darkness, there was room for her.

He said, "Maybe you could go back to the start. You can warn people...If they don't listen, at least find me. I was still a person then.

Tell me. We'll see what we can do. Maybe we can save humanity. Tell me. I will always listen to you, Carla."

O

THE LAST PAPER STARS
written by Allen Frost

The Last Frankenstein (1991)
Paper Guide (1997)
Stars Become Sand When They Land (1990)

Books by Good Deed Rain

Saint Lemonade, Allen Frost, 2014. Two novels illustrated by the author in the manner of the old Big Little Books.

Playground, Allen Frost, 2014. Poems collected from seven years of chapbooks.

Roosevelt, Allen Frost, 2015. A Pacific Northwest novel set in July, 1942, when a boy and a girl search for a missing elephant. Illustrated throughout by Fred Sodt.

5 Novels, Allen Frost, 2015. Novels written over five years, featuring circus giants, clockwork animals, detectives and time travelers.

The Sylvan Moore Show, Allen Frost, 2015. A short story omnibus of 193 stories written over 30 years.

Town in a Cloud, Allen Frost, 2015. A 3 part book of poetry, written during the Bellingham rainy seasons of fall, winter, and spring.

A Flutter of Birds Passing Through Heaven: A Tribute to Robert Sund. 2016. Edited by Allen Frost and Paul Piper. The story of a legendary Ish River poet & artist.

At the Edge of America, Allen Frost, 2016. Two novels in one book blend time travel in a mythical poetic America.

Lake Erie Submarine, Allen Frost, 2016. A two week vacation in Ohio inspired these poems, illustrated by the author.

and Light, Paul Piper, 2016. Poetry written over three years. Illustrated with watercolors by Penny Piper.

The Book of Ticks, Allen Frost, 2017. A giant collection of 8 mysterious adventures featuring Phil Ticks. Illustrated throughout by Aaron Gunderson.

I Can Only Imagine, Allen Frost, 2017. Five adventures of love and heartbreak dreamed in an imaginary world. Cover & color illustrations by Annabelle Barrett.

The Orphanage of Abandoned Teenagers, Allen Frost, 2017. A fictional guide for teens and their parents. Illustrated by the author.

In the Valley of Mystic Light: An Oral History of the Skagit Valley Arts Scene, 2017. Edited by Claire Swedberg & Rita Hupy.

Different Planet, Allen Frost, 2017. Four science fiction adventures: reincarnation, robots, talking animals, outer space and clones. Cover & illustrations by Laura Vasyutynska.

Go with the Flow: A Tribute to Clyde Sanborn. 2018. Edited by Allen Frost. The life and art of a timeless river poet.

Homeless Sutra, Allen Frost, 2018. Four stories: Sylvan Moore, a flying monk, a water salesman, and a guardian rabbit.

The Lake Walker, Allen Frost 2018. A little novel set in black and white like one of those old European movies about death and life.

A Hundred Dreams Ago, Allen Frost, 2018. A winter book of poetry and prose. Illustrated by Aaron Gunderson.

Almost Animals, Allen Frost, 2018. A collection of linked stories, thinking about what makes us animals.

The Robotic Age, Allen Frost, 2018. A vaudeville magician and his robot track down ghosts. Illustrated throughout by Aaron Gunderson.

Kennedy, Allen Frost, 2018. This sequel to Roosevelt is a coming-of-age fable set during two weeks in 1962 in a mythical Kennedy-land. Illustrated throughout by Fred Sodt.

Fable, Allen Frost, 2018. There's something going on in this country and I can best relate it in fable: the parable of the rabbits, a bedtime story, and the diary of our trip to Ohio.

Elbows & Knees: Essays & Plays, Allen Frost, 2018. A thrilling collection of writing about some of my favorite subjects, from B-movies to Brautigan.

The Last Paper Stars, Allen Frost 2019. A trip back in time to the 20 year old mind of Frankenstein, and two other worlds of the future.

good deed rain

www.ingramcontent.com/pod-product-compliance
Lightning Source LLC
Chambersburg PA
CBHW050301110726
47898CB00007B/2485